AND

FLESH

M. DARUSHA WEHM

Pixels and Flesh
an Andersson Dexter novel
by M. Darusha Wehm

Copyright 2017 M. Darusha Wehm

Published by *in potentia* press

ISBN 978-0- 9941332-9-8

Science Fiction Books by M. Darusha Wehm

Beautiful Red
Children of Arkadia

The Andersson Dexter series:

Self Made
Act of Will
The Beauty of Our Weapons
Pixels and Flesh

Mainstream Books by Darusha Wehm

The Home for Wayward Parrots (forthcoming)

The Devi Jones' Locker series:

Packet Trade
Sea Change
Storm Cloud
Floating Point

One

"ANDERSSON DEXTER. IT'S BEEN A WHILE."

Dex looked up at the sound of a familiar voice and his face broke into a smile. He jumped up from behind his desk and in a couple of long strides had rounded it and come face to face with his visitor. Virtual face to virtual face, of course, as this surprise visit was taking place in Dex's office in Marionette City. Still, even if it was only a simulation, Dex was happy to see his old friend and mentor, Zahara Zhang.

"Zizou!" He opened his arms in a hug-or-handshake shape and waited for Zhang to choose one. She stepped into his embrace and gave Dex a quick squeeze. "What brings you over here?"

"Would you believe me if I said I just wanted to say hi?"

Dex's former boss rarely gave away much on her face, and she didn't now, but Dex knew she wasn't really trying to fool him.

"Nope," he said, sliding back into his overstuffed brown tweed chair and leaning back. He smiled as the chair squeaked slightly at his weight. His office space was an unusually robust simulation; enough to almost make him feel like it was real. He gestured at the visitor's chair across the desk and Zhang sat. "So, what's up, Cap?"

"I haven't been your captain in a long while," Zhang said.

"Old habits die hard," Dex answered, "and while I'd be perfectly happy to shoot the shit with you all day, I don't recall that exactly being your style." He leaned forward, a hint of a frown creasing his avatar's forehead. "Is everything okay?"

Zhang nodded, then shrugged. "I think so? It's just... something particularly weird has happened. And I have to admit that the first person I think of when I think 'particularly weird' is you. So here I am."

Dex could tell that Captain Zhang was going to tell her story in her own time, and her reluctance to just be out with it aroused his curiosity more than her vague explanations. He knew her well enough after working for her for years that pushing was pointless, so he opened up the lower right drawer of his desk and removed a half-empty bottle of whiskey and a pair of short glasses. It was a flavour-only formulation, neurostim not being Dex's first choice for mood alteration. Besides, he was working.

He lifted the bottle in a silent question and Zhang nodded. Dex poured two rounds and passed one across the desk. Zhang took it and clinked her glass against the one in Dex's hand. They each took a sip, then Zhang set her glass on the desk and reached into the inside left pocket of her suit coat.

She pulled out a folded sheaf of papers and passed them across the desk to Dex. She'd forwarded him the file on an encrypted private channel, but the program which generated the illusion of his office rendered all of Dex's online activities into their analog counterparts. His avatar took the papers and Dex skimmed the contents.

"I'm no lawyer," he said, "but if I understand this at all, you've just come into quite the inheritance. An entire disk block of rez space in the Cuba Quarter? That must be worth a fortune. Congratulations! And condolences," he added after a short but awkward pause.

Zhang nodded, her lips set in a tight line. "Thanks, but condolences aren't exactly required." She pointed at the name listed on the documents. Irina Nightingale, Zhang's late benefactor. "I have never heard of this person before in my life."

"WELL, HOW ABOUT SOMEONE the squad helped?" Dex suggested. "Maybe it's not for you, specifically, but what you represent?"

Dex had refilled their glasses as they went over the obvious — a long, lost relative or someone Zhang had known under another name. Of course, she had already thought of those possibilities and her own investigation had come up with no connection to Nightingale.

Zhang nodded, but said, "I couldn't find any record of Nightingale in any of our files. Besides, why name me personally in the will, if that's the reason? And how would someone even get my name? I can't even remember the last time I dealt directly with one of our cases." A look crossed her face and Dex guessed that she had been inadvertently including him in that "our." He had worked as a member of the detective squad overseen by Zahara Zhang until he had been transferred to his current unit, which dealt with cases that took place in the virtual world.

That thought tweaked something in his brain and he detoured the conversation. "You think this is something to do with M City?"

Zhang followed the abrupt change of tack easily. "Not specifically. Why?"

"Well," Dex said, "isn't that why you're here? I mean, I know I'm the greatest detective that ever was, but surely there are still detectives on your patch who can look into this for you?"

Zhang laughed at Dex's false immodesty. "We are somehow managing to scrape by without you, it's true," she said, then her smile faded. "The real truth is I didn't want to give this to the squad. I know how this works, and since I haven't managed to figure out the connection it means there's something... complicated going on here. And complicated usually means personal, and personal..."

Dex lifted his glass in acknowledgment. "Say no more. I'll look into it. And, Cap, thanks for trusting me with, well, wherever this ends up."

Zhang nodded. "Feel free to bring Lewis into this, too."

"You know I can't keep much from her for long," Dex grinned.

"Besides," Zhang said, taking the whisky bottle and pouring them both a top-up, "if you can't trust your revolutionary collaborators, who can you trust?"

WHEN DEX LINKED OUT of M City and refocussed on the physical world he felt the worse for wear. He'd gotten used to long hours online and was even starting to feel comfortable in the repurposed closet he used as a home office. When he was online he didn't need much space — he'd never gotten the hang of moving in a three-D rendered simulation online while still walking around the physical world, so he liked to find a comfortable spot and just sit when he was online. His old apartment was tiny, built for one, and he used the only chair in the place for the job. But now, that was no longer an option.

He stood and shook the kinks out of his body and slid open the door after knocking on it. If Annabelle was home he knew she'd appreciate the brief warning that he was about to reappear in their shared space. Dex stepped into their living room and didn't see her there or through the open bedroom door, so he deduced that she must be out.

I'm the greatest detective that ever was, he thought to himself and chuckled. The apartment he shared with his partner in crime and life was a palace compared to everywhere else he'd ever lived, but it was still small enough to know immediately if there was anyone else home. There obviously wasn't.

Dex performed his usual post-online routine: toilet, glass of water, food brick, look out the window. Evening was setting in, the sinking Mediterranean sun casting a luminous glow over Nice. It was beautiful, so beautiful that Dex wondered for what must have been the millionth time why anyone would ever have thought to create a virtual world in the first place.

He breathed deeply of the slightly salty air, remembering that he was profoundly lucky. Only a few years previously he'd lived in a grimy, grey, cell-like apartment, in a grimy, grey city. It had been a grimy, grey existence from which Dex knew he'd escaped due to no real merit on his part. He'd fallen in with a good crowd, was all. Luck had more to do with it than anything else.

It was dreadfully unfair.

He was so caught up in his thoughts that he physically jumped when he heard the soft *snick* of the lock slide back.

"Hey," a tired-sounding Annabelle said as she came into the apartment. She looked sweaty and a bit dishevelled and it had been months since she'd changed her hair, but she looked wonderful to Dex. He kept to the other side of the apartment, waiting for her to come to him if she was going to. Ever since Omnitrack determined that all employees had to physically go into their offices to work, Annabelle had been forced to go out into the physical world more days than not. It was, to put it mildly, not her favourite thing to do.

"I just got back myself," Dex said, keeping himself still. "You need anything? Food?"

Annabelle shook her head and took a few steps into the apartment. She approached Dex, kissed him lightly, then backed away again. There was a time when that would have been far more contact than she could handle after a whole day out in the physical world, but there was also a time when the idea that the two of them would share a home full-time was beyond laughable.

"I'm not hungry. Just beat." She flopped onto the chaise longue and closed her eyes.

Dex let her sit for a moment, then slipped into the bedroom. He quickly changed into a clean outfit and called from the doorway, "I could use a walk. I'll get out of your hair for a little while?"

Annabelle murmured something unintelligible that Dex took to be the sound of agreement. Then she said clearly, "Want to meet at Monte's in a bit? Say half an hour?"

Dex smiled to himself. "You bet, kiddo. See you there."

Dex quietly left the apartment and spiralled down to the ground floor. He really did want to stretch his legs, but half an hour would be enough. He could take the long way to his favourite bar and link into M City from there. It hardly even seemed odd to him anymore — sitting in a real world bar full of other real world humans, but focussing on a virtual bar to meet the avatar of the woman with whom he shared a home.

It was just modern living.

ONE OF LE RÉTRO'S human servers brought Dex his glass of rum and water, setting it on the table in front of him with a smile.

"Not meeting anyone today?" the waiter asked. Dex was a regular and usually sat in the main bar area with one or more friends or colleagues. Tonight he took one of the small one-person booths along the wall which catered to people who intended to log into the 'nets. Thanks to the everywherenet backbone that a consortium of the largest companies maintained, there was hardly anywhere a person couldn't log in, so most places expected at least a portion of their customers would be only partially present.

"Had to get out of the house for a while," he answered, "but my date's waiting for me online."

The waiter gave Dex a knowing smile and said, "I'll leave you to it, then." Dex took a sip of his drink, unfocussed his eyes from the bar in which his body sat and linked into Three Card Monte's.

From one ginmill to another, he thought as the M City bar and his longtime hangout seemed to materialize before him. His avatar instantiated at a table, and not long later a virtual drink, ashtray and pack of cigarettes appeared. It was all an affectation, no different from his avatar's charcoal suit and the felt hat he dropped onto the table. He'd just lit a cigarette when Annabelle walked into the bar.

Her avatar was a reasonable replica of her physical world appearance, without the tiredness. She made a bee line for Dex's table, and in contrast to her greeting at the apartment, favoured Dex with a long, deep kiss. She settled in to the bench seat next to him and snuggled close.

"What a shit of a day," she said once she'd had a deep draught of her own virtual drink.

"What happened?" Dex asked but Annabelle shook her head.

"Nothing special, just the same old crap." She turned to look at him. "Was there really ever a time I actually liked my job?"

He laughed, though it wasn't particularly funny. She had liked, maybe even loved her work at Omnitrack once. But in the last few years things had gotten more and more difficult, not just for Annabelle, but for everyone who worked for the major firms.

The worst part was that Dex was entirely certain that it was because of him.

TWO

"IT'S NOT LIKE WE DIDN'T know that creating a distributed version of the 'nets that the firms can't control was going to piss them off," Annabelle said. "Of course, they are going to fight to hang on to their business interests. That they were completely fucking up M City in their little wars to take over each other's markets was what got this whole ball rolling in the first place. You know that." She took Dex's hand in hers and leaned in. "*They* started this."

"I know. I just—" Dex sighed. "I just wonder if I could have found a better way, some solution that would have protected M City without making everything so shitty for everyone out there." He gestured to the door of Monte's but he was sure Annabelle knew he was referring to the physical world.

"Dex," Annabelle softened her voice. "I appreciate your sense of personal responsibility, but it's edging a little close to megalomania. If I remember correctly, I was the one who helped write the package that took this away from the firms, not you." She spread her arms in an all-encompassing gesture. "And I don't regret it for a hot second."

Dex lit a cigarette and pondered. She was right, of course.

"I guess I always knew that there would be consequences, unintended side effects. I just didn't think it would be this."

This was more than employers forcing people to physically go into work. It was what had become a deep division between those who were loyal to their employers and the system of anarcho-capitalism which ruled most of the world, and the people who were actively resisting the status quo. Resisters like Dex, who worked as a freelancer based in M City, and like Annabelle, who held a regular corporate job but moonlighted with online or freelance work, or spent their personal time in M City.

The virtual world had developed a robust society complete with businesses, communities, and social groups. When that had been threatened, a diverse cross-section of people joined together to keep their online space alive. It had worked — perhaps too well. The mega-firms which controlled business in the physical world had recognized this as a threat to their supremacy and economic battle lines were drawn. Ordinary people trying to make ends meet were the first casualties.

"It's going to get worse before it gets better, Dex." Annabelle finished her drink and another materialized on the table. "This was never going to be a once-and-done. It's just the start."

"Yeah, I know. I only hope it does get better."

She took his hand and squeezed. The sensation progressed through Dex's implants and his real hand felt almost as if she were really there next to him in Le Rétro.

"Enough depressing state-of-the-world talk," she said, leaving her hand on his. "I've been so swamped at Omnitrack, I haven't hit the squad boards in months. What's new in Mack Larsen's Band of Merry Avatars?"

Dex groaned. He still held an unjustified dislike of his boss, and seeing his old captain again had only reawakened those negative feelings. "Nothing interesting," he said, reaching for his drink in both the physical and virtual bars. "You haven't missed much. At least Larsen hasn't taken a page out of the corporate playbook and made us all start going into that chrome and glass monstrosity he calls a squad room."

Annabelle laughed and shook her head. "I've never understood why you hate that building so much."

Dex shrugged and looked around at Monte's with its low-lying cloud of blue smoke, dark wood panelling and lurid red leather booths. "This is more my style."

"You are such an anachronism," Annabelle said, "but I wouldn't have you any other way."

Annabelle ordered a plate of virtual snacks and Dex felt his stomach growl. "Give me a minute?" he asked and Annabelle nodded.

Dex left this avatar running in Monte's but refocussed on Le Rétro. He flagged down the server and ordered a refill and a food brick. He didn't mind paying for the space and ambiance with a drink or two, but it bugged him to pay double for the moulded nutrient supplements he had a case of back at the apartment. He rationalized it as a small price to pay to keep his relationship with Annabelle functional.

He had grown to appreciate M City on an aesthetic and practical level, but would honestly have been happy enough to never leave the physical world. Annabelle, on the other hand... Dex often replayed the context of their last serious argument. If she could live her entire life permanently in a simulation, she would choose that in a second. He knew that nothing would stop her — not him, not anything. It was only a case of the technology being out of reach that kept her physically embodied. So, he accommodated her need to escape the physical world, to meet her at least half way between pixels and flesh.

His order arrived and he ate half the mushy food substitute in a couple of bites. He washed down the meal with his watered-down rum and re-animated his avatar.

"Better?" Annabelle asked.

Dex nodded and picked up one of the deep-fried morsels from the snacks plate. He could taste it, and nearly feel the crunch in his mouth. One day he might even get used to the sensation.

"So, how was your day?"

"Pretty damn interesting, actually," Dex said. "Guess who came into my office today?"

Annabelle raised an eyebrow. "Some long cool drink of water, looking like trouble on two legs, with a desperate tale to melt your jaded detective heart?"

"I think she'd punch you in the face if she heard you describe her that way," Dex said, laughing. "It was Captain Zhang."

Annabelle's mouth literally fell open. "Zizou. In your office? Is she trying to get you back from Larsen after all?"

"Sadly, no. It's a... personal matter."

"Okay, now you've really got my interest piqued. I mean, I'm not going to ask you to break confidentiality or anything, but..." Her eyes were wide. "Can you tell me?"

Dex grinned. "As tempting as it would be to make you froth at the mouth in curiosity, the Cap said I could loop you in."

Dex gave her a brief run-down on the captain's mysterious stroke of good fortune.

"And she has no idea who this person is?"

"Nope," Dex confirmed.

"Any chance it's a mistake," Annabelle asked. "The wrong Zahara Zhang, maybe?"

Dex shook his head. "The paperwork is very clear. It's Zizou, all right."

"Well," Annabelle said, grinning. "It doesn't sound easy, but at least you won't be bored."

WHEN DEX GOT BACK to the apartment, Annabelle was in bed. She must have heard him come in, since she called out, "Come on in. I'm just reading."

Dex got himself ready for bed and slid in next to her. She was still online, her eyes unfocussed. He waited on his side of the bed, knowing she might or might not come over. It was fine either way — just having her weight next to him was a tangible proof of her comfort with him. After a few minutes she blinked a couple of times and looked over at him.

"I'm beat," she said, with an apologetic smile.

"Me, too."

She leaned over and gave Dex a quick kiss, then lay down and the lights dimmed. "I love you," she murmured into her pillow.

"Love you, too, kiddo," Dex said as he closed his eyes, a contented smile on his face.

DEX HAD HIS VIRTUAL feet up on his virtual desk when the phone rang. The shrill tone startled him, and he scowled at the annoyance. He lifted the heavy black handset and said aloud, "This is Dex, go."

"You were right."

The voice of Mack Larsen, Dex's current captain, never failed to put Dex in a foul mood. Even when Larsen was complimenting his work.

"Sir?" For some twisted reason, Dex might have been even more annoyed at Larsen being nice to him. There was something about the captain that inherently pissed Dex off and while he knew it was irrational and inappropriate, he couldn't help himself.

"Tapping into the feeds from Sim's Stims worked a charm. We've got those hoods dead to rights." Dex knew without looking it up which case Larsen referred to. In the wake of the organized vandalism of the virtual world at the hands of some the large companies, a few enterprising low-lifes had started a copy-cat extortion business. Larsen's squad had been investigating an online stim supplier whose storefront had been repeatedly attacked with some poorly executed but still bothersome malware. After a couple of attacks, the ransom demand had arrived.

Dex had suggested that the supplier allow the squad to monitor a live feed from their instantiation. It was a pain and an invasion of their privacy, but they'd been willing to try. It had only been a few days since they began monitoring, and now Larsen was calling with the good news.

"Glad to hear it," Dex said. "You sending over some goons to roust them?"

Dex could somehow hear the grin in Larsen's voice. "Thought you might want to get your hands dirty."

It would be a lot easier if I could learn to like this man, Dex thought. He really isn't that bad a guy.

"Yeah. I would, at that," he said aloud. "Thanks, boss."

Larsen sent the details about the culprits to Dex's system, which appeared as a manila folder materializing in Dex's in tray. He picked it up and flicked through the photos and papers stuffed inside. "I'll get right on this."

DEX LINKED OVER TO a public portal in the Zubers block. The information Larsen had sent over showed that the would-be shake-down artists frequented a music and stims hangout in the area. A quick look at the user list for the area showed that they were online and nearby. Dex found the bar and entered, keeping his avatar hidden. He scanned the room and found his quarry at a back booth, the two avatars laughing and sharing a stim pipe.

Dex accessed his onboard system and found a nasty little bit of code Annabelle had written years ago. Dex didn't understand how it worked, but he knew from experience that when he sent it to another avatar it would appear as a benign, but annoying image — like an insect or bit of fluff. Most people instinctively brushed it away, and when their avatars touched it, the payload was injected into their systems. It wasn't permanent — the rendering system was designed to be self-correcting and the effects would wear off in a few minutes, but for a moment, any affected avatar would be paralyzed.

Dex made his avatar visible and strode toward the now-frozen hoodlums.

"Not so much fun to be on the boot end of the kicking, is it?" he growled. "But if you lie down in malware, you can't be too surprised when you wake up with broken pixels, can you?"

He almost wished that the frozen effect had worn off,

because there was no reaction to his words. He figured that he was getting through, though. This little trick usually worked a charm. He sat down at the table across from them, and leaned in.

"What is wrong with you, anyway? With everything going on in here, the last thing we need to be doing is turning on each other. You really think that the graft you can get from shaking down a mom-and-pop stim joint is going to elevate you into the financial stratosphere? If the firms end up destroying M City in their turf wars, do you honestly thing a few extra euros will make any difference to you? All you're doing is making it easier for our real enemies to destroy us."

The avatar on the left, a blue-spotted humanoid with feathers, began to stir. "You got us, old man," a high-pitched voice came out of the jerky, pixellated avatar. "But you're wrong. Wrong about the firms and wrong about M City. You want to think that we're all alike, that all of us who live online want the same things, but you don't know us. You don't know who we are, what we want. If you think there's some kind of united resistance, some allegiance to your precious "Mission" in here, well. Then you're even dumber than some stim jockey who can't even secure their code."

Their paralysis had completely worn off now, because both avatars dematerialized. Dex sat at the table, staring at the empty space where they'd been. He was pretty sure that his message had gotten through and they wouldn't be bothering Sim's Stims any more. This had been a warning, a harmless demonstration of what else could be possible, and they knew it as well as he did. But what Feathers had said got to him.

Because it wasn't wrong.

THREE

DEX WALKED OUT THE door of the stim joint, and pointed his avatar in the direction of his virtual office in the Chandlers district. If he walked the whole way it would take him close to an hour, and he could have linked back instantly, but walking always helped him clear his head. It didn't seem to matter whether the feet beating the streets were physical or not.

As he walked past the storefronts, public art, and social spaces, Dex noted that most of the simulated buildings had a small red flower displayed somewhere — on the "open" sign, in a window, as graffiti. The symbol indicated that the space was protected using the system that Annabelle and others had developed to distribute the code that generated M City among the people who inhabited the virtual world, rather than relying completely on the firms which provided the network. In recent years, the red flower had become nearly as ubiquitous as the double gold coin symbol indicating that goods could be purchased though anonymous cash transfer.

Seeing all those red flowers, a person could be forgiven for thinking that M City was a united community. If Dex only counted the people who ran independent businesses based online, it might even be close to true. But the vast majority of

M City users were just regular folks. People who, in the physical world, held regular corporate jobs, with employer-supplied housing and other basics. Dex had been one of them once. Annabelle was still one of them. She held a high level position, so her housing allowance was larger than most and she earned enough on top of the benefits to supplement her food or housing rations if she wanted to. Most people weren't so fortunate and had to make do on the basics.

Since net access was an essential service and almost every job required networked implants, going online was as easy as walking across the street. For most people, hanging out online was cheaper than socializing in the physical world. Basically, unless you were rich, you hung out in M City.

Dex stopped paying attention to the stuff of the virtual world and looked around at the avatars. At the *people*. There were a lot more users in the area than he could see reflected in the various bodies on the street. His penchant for walking was unusual, but even so, he passed several other avatars moving around the old-fashioned way. Most were of the same ilk as Dex's — human-looking, attired in something the owner likely considered to be aesthetically pleasing. Of those, the vast majority were of a type that most would find attractive, though there were always a few who broke the mould — avatars styled to look like children or old people, some clearly designed to appear intimidating or even frightening. There were also the ones which were more fantastic: animals based on real or fantasy creatures, robots, aliens, some things Dex couldn't even begin to explain.

It was a typical cross-section of M City life, as ordinary as dirt.

After about fifteen minutes of introspection, Dex

abandoned his walk and linked back into his office. He filed his report for Captain Larsen about his little chat with the putative extortioners, suggesting that a similar conversation in the physical world by the local goon squad wouldn't go amiss. He knew that Larsen would likely already be in touch with the relevant team, but it never hurt to make a complete report.

It make him wonder. An amateur-hour shakedown wasn't in any of the firms' usual repertoires, and he didn't really think Feathers was on anyone's payroll. But he didn't know. They could be anyone.

All the avatars he'd passed on his walk were essentially anonymous. Any of them could be spying for one of the firms or for the everywherenet consortium. And even if they weren't spies, who was to say where someone's allegiances lay? Loyalty to an employer wasn't entirely outdated, and enough people would be motivated to ensure that their meal tickets weren't revoked. Feathers was right — there might be a battle going on, but unless you knew someone well, there was no way to be sure which side they would be on.

Dex was spared having to think about this too hard by the bleating of his telephone. The sound was uniquely annoying but he loved it. He loved all the subtle touches of anachronism that Annabelle had put into the instantiation of his office. Each time Dex looked out the window at the simulated view, whenever he heard his chair creak when he leaned back, and every time the phone rang, he was reminded of how much Annabelle loved him.

"This is Dex, go," he said roughly into the black handset. He might be full of warm thoughts about Annabelle, but that didn't affect his professional demeanour.

"Andersson Dexter," the silky smooth voice at the other

end of the line said, "why is it that I have not seen your face in... well, it seems like an age?"

"Biagini," Dex grinned and lost his professional surliness. "Surely you aren't tired of your latest sweetheart already?"

"That's sweethearts *plural*, I'll have you know. And of course not, but there is something to be said for spending time with the one person alive immune to my charms."

Dex laughed. Nearly everything René Biagini said was an exaggeration at best — well, probably not the plural sweethearts. But René and Dex were close only in a platonic way, and notwithstanding Biagini's inability to avoid flirtation, both intended to keep it that way. Biagini would have been happy to add a professional element — he was Zahara Zhang's local counterpart. But when Dex was transferred to Larsen's unit, Biagini had to accept that it was not to be. It was yet another area over which the two men bonded.

Dex flipped through the files in his inbox. His report to Larsen complete, the only thing left on his plate was Zizou's mystery inheritance and he was still mulling it over. He knew his method was inefficient, but his years of experience told him that there was no point to diving in without a plan. His mind needed to chew over a tough case, his subconscious performing its background machinations before he could get started.

"I suppose I could be induced into taking a break."

"Lunch at Le Rétro?"

Dex grimaced. Since moving in with Annabelle, he'd become much more cognizant of the amount of money he spent on physical world luxuries. He'd been at the café only the previous day and felt guilty about returning again so soon.

"How about the plaza by Liberté?" he suggested instead. "Save a few pennies."

"Sure," Biagini said. "See you there in thirty minutes?"

Dex grunted his assent and broke the connection. It really had been a while since he'd caught up with René. He wondered why that might be.

DEX SPIRALLED DOWN TO the ground floor and walked out into the bright afternoon sun. He squinted against the light and saw that he'd beaten his friend to the park. It wasn't terribly surprising, since it was literally outside his front door. As usual, there were more people relaxing on the benches and lawn here than there had been avatars on Dex's Zubers walk, but only a few more. Early evening tended to see much more use of the community space, with groups of Dex's neighbours playing games, sharing meals, or even holding impromptu concerts. Dex sometimes joined them on his cheap mandolin, but he realized that he couldn't remember the last time that had happened, either.

What was up with him? Had he somehow reverted to his old, unhealthy, loner behaviour? He certainly didn't feel like he used to back in the bad old days.

"Are you online?" Biagini's voice startled Dex but he recovered quickly and the two shared a warm embrace.

"Why did you think I was online?" Dex asked as they disengaged and sat on a nearby bench.

"You had the thousand metre stare," Biagini said.

Dex nodded. "Thinking."

"Mmm. An interesting case, I presume."

"Yes and no," Dex said. "I do have an interesting case, but that's not what was on my mind."

"Oh?" Biagini's left eyebrow shot up, but he didn't elaborate any further. It was a method of enquiry which worked surprisingly well.

"René, tell me something. Have I been... Do I seem..." Dex trailed off and Biagini did the eyebrow trick again. Dex laughed. "It just occurred to me that I haven't been doing a lot of the things I used to do. You know, for fun. I don't remember the last time I came down here to jam with Zeke and Noemi. Chemical Celeste hasn't played a gig in months. And it *has* been 'an age' since you and I got together." He made finger quotes around René's odd turn of phrase.

Dex looked across the plaza, at one small group of people exercising together, another trio having a picnic on the grass.

"Have I gone back to being a lonely, sad sack cliché?"

"Do you feel lonely?" Biagini asked after a short pause. "Do you feel sad?"

"Not at all! Quite the opposite. But I didn't see it coming when it happened before. What if I'm regressing and I just can't tell?"

René thought for a moment, then a slight smile tugged at the corner of his mouth. "About how long do you think it's been?" he asked. "Roughly speaking."

Dex did the mental arithmetic. "I guess the last time I came down for a music night was... shit, it must be nearly six months ago!"

"And did anything else happen around then? Any significant changes?"

"Well, that was around when Annabelle and I moved in toge—"

Biagini laughed and put his arm around Dex, whose mouth was hanging open. "You are *nesting*, mon ami. Making a home sweet home with your lady love. It is exactly to be expected. But," Biagini's grip on Dex's shoulder increased slightly, "it is not to last forever. We must do more of this, you and I, and it is probably about time to perpetrate one of your evenings of caterwauling noise, as well."

"Can I expect to see you in the audience, old friend?" Dex asked, laughing.

Biagini gave his head a curt shake. "This is not an emergency situation, not yet. You are fine, just don't get too comfortable, will you? Miss Annabelle must be willing to share you with the rest of us, at least a little."

"Are you two taking my name in vain?" Dex turned around to see Annabelle coming toward them, a smirk on her face.

"Never," Biagini said with mock outrage. "I was just reminding your paramour here that there is a whole world beyond your boudoir."

A pink flush tinted Annabelle's cheeks, but she said, "You are terrible, René Biagini. If I thought it were possible, I'd say you're a bad influence."

"Hard as it may be to imagine," Dex said, "it's quite the opposite."

"Well, after all this praise I best leave before I become an incorrigible egoist." Biagini stood and opened his arms.

Dex walked into the embrace, saying, "More incorrigible, you mean?"

"The two of you deserve each other," Annabelle said, tuning to head toward the building. "See you in a few minutes."

Dex nodded and watched her walk away.

"I don't deserve *her*," he said once Annabelle was out of earshot.

"And what a wonder it is," Biagini said, with a wistful smile, "that she disagrees."

The warm feeling spreading through Dex's chest chilled as the unmistakable sound of an explosion shattered the peaceful calm of the Mediterranean evening.

FOUR

"GET DOWN!"

Dex felt the full weight of René Biagini on him, as the other man hauled them both to the ground. Screams and the sound of panic surrounded them, but Dex didn't see any indication that whatever had occurred was near them. He extricated himself from under Biagini and carefully looked around. The crowds of people in the plaza had disbursed, but otherwise Dex couldn't see anything obviously untoward.

Dex was getting his breathing under control when his heart rate leapt up again at the sight of Annabelle running from the front door of Liberté. He scrambled to his feet and ran toward her, ignoring the sound of Biagini's protests.

"Are you okay?" they both shouted as they neared each other, then collided in a tight embrace.

"I'm fine," Dex got out first. "You?"

He could feel Annabelle nod and then she pulled away from him. "I couldn't tell how close it was," she said. "Training just kicked in, I guess."

Annabelle had briefly been in the military, when she'd worn a different body and hadn't yet understood that it was the flesh that needed to change, rather than her sense of who she was. It had been a lifetime ago, but the training was designed to become automatic, and this wasn't the first time she'd acted without thinking. It always affected her badly.

Dex watched her closely as the adrenaline wore off, and as she began to tremble he led her to the bench where Biagini now sat, his eyes unfocussed as he doubtlessly was online trying to learn what had happened. Dex helped Annabelle sit and once she had her head between her knees and was breathing evenly, he went online himself.

The news feeds scrolling across his vision didn't tell him anything useful — it was either information he already knew or dangerously wild speculation. Political terrorists, renegade streeters, rival firms. All plausible enough, but it was too soon for any of those theories to be proved. But nothing boosted a media stream's readership like a juicy catastrophe, the more incendiary the better.

He paged over to the internal communications network for Larsen's squad. It was one of the decentralized units that made up a global network of security personnel who dealt with issues that the firms' internal security forces wouldn't address. Each unit acted more or less independently, but they shared information and resources. Dex quickly scrolled through the real time descriptions and images from the scene.

"Do they know what happened?" Annabelle's voice was muffled.

"It was the power bank at de Gaulle," Biagini said, referring to a small park several blocks away. "Don't know if it was deliberate or not."

The large blocks of batteries which stored solar, wind and tidal energy were generally safe, but nothing is foolproof.

"The power bank," Annabelle said, slowing sitting up.

"Surely that would have just been a pop and a fire? We'd never have heard it all the way here."

Dex scanned through the reports. "Someone here thinks that the power bank went off and the resulting fire spread to some construction materials being stored nearby, which was what actually detonated."

"It looks mighty suspicious," Biagini said.

"Maybe," Dex shrugged. "If I were trying to blow up a block of Nice, I don't think I'd rely on a power bank overcharging for my detonator."

"Uh, fellas," Annabelle said, and Dex looked over to see her face was ashen. "Casualties?"

"Oh, honey, I'm sorry," Dex said. "I forgot that you're not seeing what we're seeing." He sat next to her and took her hand. "It doesn't look like there's anything serious. A few scrapes and bruises — one person got burned but it's nothing a few hours in a med clinic won't solve."

She let out a breath and seemed to deflate but a bit of colour came back to her cheeks. "Well, that's good news, at least."

"Now we have to hope it stays that way," René said darkly.

"What do you mean?" Dex asked. "Everything has been contained on the scene."

Biagini shook his head. "I'm not talking about de Gaulle," he said. "People are afraid. And between being afraid and some of the ridiculous things I'm seeing on the feeds... well, I just hope that no one decides that this is something that needs to be avenged." He frowned. "Or copied."

DEX TOOK ANNABELLE UP to their apartment and spent a

few minutes fussing over her.

"I'm fine," she protested after a third offer of food and shot him a glare. "What I really need now is a bit of peace and quiet."

That meant solitude. Being left alone was the last thing in the world Dex would have wanted if he'd had her reaction, but he'd learned a long time ago that the trick wasn't to treat people the way you wanted to be treated, it was to treat them the way *they* wanted to be treated.

"I hear you," he said and gave her a quick kiss on the cheek. "Ping me if you need anything." She nodded, a visible look of relief on her face as Dex stepped into the hallway. That reaction would never stop hurting, but he knew that wasn't the intent. As it was, Dex didn't want to be on his own, so he checked into the local squad as he spiralled down the lift. He didn't expect they needed more bodies at the scene and he couldn't imagine how he'd be particularly useful, but there must be something he could do.

As the squad captain, Biagini would have his hands full, but Dex had met a few of Biagini's people over the past few years. As he stepped out into the courtyard, he scrolled through the short list of his local contacts. Most of them were showing busy, but Jamie Eristo's name was illuminated in green. Dex had only met Jamie a few times, but they'd gotten along well enough. It would have to do.

"Dex!" Jamie's voice sounded in Dex's ear. "Everything all right where you are?"

"Fine, Jamie. I was with René over at Liberté and we heard it go off. How about you?"

"I only found out about it from the feeds. I was down the coast, but I'm on my way back now. Should be at Gare de Ville in ten minutes. Want to meet up?"

Dex smiled. "Yeah. I don't know if we can be useful..."

"...but it's better than doing nothing!"

"Amen to that."

❖❖❖❖❖

DEX RECOGNIZED JAMIE EASILY at the train station. They were unusually tall, with the slim build, youthful features and clear skin of most people who lived off the nutritionally balanced supplements provided by the firms. Food bricks would never win any culinary awards, but they kept you alive, healthy and young — at least until they didn't any more.

Dex waved and waited until recognition dawned on Jamie's face. They strode toward Dex and stuck out a hand for a firm shake.

"You're a detective on the M City squad, right?"

Dex nodded as the two set off out of the train station.

"Any theories?"

Dex pursed his lips. "Not really. From what I know, it could just be an accident."

Jamie barked a short laugh. "I'm no fan of coincidences, Dex."

"Neither am I," Dex said, "but an accident would be the simplest explanation."

Jamie grunted and Dex wondered if he'd made a mistake in reaching out. "Maybe, but after everything else that's been going on, it's hard to just accept this as an unrelated event."

"Wait a minute," Dex said, stopping in the middle of the sidewalk. "What 'everything else'?"

"Of course," Jamie said, with something approximating a smile appearing on their face. "You're not Nice squad. You won't see the dailies — you don't know."

"Know what?"

Jamie blinked rapidly a few times, then said, "Let me show you."

A fraction of a second passed, then Dex felt the weight of a message hitting his system. He unfocussed and opened up the link from Jamie. At first it reminded Dex of the usual reports from an urban squad. Shakedowns, petty theft, the odd spot of vandalism. Nothing he hadn't seen back in Namerica when he was working the streets. But then he began to see it — the pattern.

Usually this kind of crime was more or less random. Sure, the same people targeted the same areas — usually where they lived or worked. Small scale stuff like this usually was confined to the areas the firms didn't monitor — the cheap, independent housing blocks, small bars and shops. But aside from those considerations, the pattern was more or less random. They were crimes of opportunity.

This was different. The same targets were being hit over and over again, but with different events. One stim bar had their window smashed one week, was graffitied the next, had a staff member harassed, and finally was robbed of their recycling. None of these were likely to be the work of the same thugs — the recycling theft alone screamed of the work of a desperate streeter— but that the bar was repeatedly hit was unusual. And this was happening all over, at dozens of different locations.

"This..." Dex was having a hard time accepting the evidence before his eyes. "This is organized. Targeted. Jamie, what am I looking at here?"

"You know." Dex recognized the look of determination on Jamie's face. It worried him.

"You think this is a methodical intimidation campaign,"

Dex said. "Like old-fashioned organized crime?"

Jamie shrugged. "You could call it that. I'd call it terrorism."

THEY SAT AT A SMALL table in an out of the way stim bar that Jamie chose. Dex had never been there before, but it was one of a few locations outside M City which sported the red flower logo, so he assumed it would be a safe place to talk. Jamie ordered a stim cocktail, but Dex shook his head.

"You're straightedge?" Jamie asked with no hint of judgment.

"Not quite," Dex said, a smile sneaking out in spite of himself. "Stims just aren't my particular poison."

"Fair enough." They were silent as Jamie's cocktail appeared, then waited for the server to disappear.

"So," Dex said, his voice low, "you think it's political?"

"I don't know about the motivation," Jamie said, a disgusted tone on the final word. "Honestly, I hope not. This kind of thing doesn't help — it just makes everyone who speaks out against the system look bad. I get how a person could get frustrated at some corporation, but it's one thing to bust up a couple of windows, and it's another thing entirely to follow someone home from work, making it obvious you're doing it, scaring them half to death. And now this?" Jamie shook their head, a flush of anger darkening their brown skin. "Blowing shit up is some next level scumbaggery. There's no *motivation* in the world that excuses this."

Dex nodded. "But *why* is often the first clue to *who*. Or, do you already know who's behind it?"

Jamie shook their head. "To be honest, not everyone on

the squad thinks it's one group. That's my take, but there's no proof."

"Surely the douchebags doing the brickwork know who their bosses are?"

Jamie scowled and mumbled something into their cocktail.

"What's that?"

"We haven't caught anyone yet."

Dex was quiet for a moment. Your garden variety shit disturber wasn't a master criminal. Getting caught was nearly a foregone conclusion in the wake of something like a smash-and-grab. That the squad didn't have *anyone* was even more damning than the pattern. Dex could see in Jamie's expression that he was only catching up to what they already knew.

"Shit."

"Exactly."

# FIVE

JAMIE HADN'T CONVINCED DEX that the explosion was related to the rest of it, but he couldn't ignore the possibility. It was hanging out in the back of his mind while he tried to get on with the rest of his work. The next morning, there was nothing on the feeds to indicate that there was a continuing threat.

"I'll be fine," Annabelle protested. "How exactly is staying here cooped up in the apartment instead of going in to work going to make me safer from a mysterious threat that might not exist anyway?"

"You... have a point," Dex conceded.

Annabelle chuckled and kissed him on the cheek. "I know I was rattled yesterday, but the adrenaline hangover's all worn off now. In the absence of any new information, it's back to normal."

"Back to normal," Dex echoed, but he couldn't quite silence the niggling thought that something organized and dangerous was brewing.

❖◆❖◆❖

DEX LINKED INTO M CITY at the public portal in Chandlers. He walked the few blocks to the Maynard Arms, where his office was instantiated. He scanned the neighbourhood as he walked, not looking for anything in particular, just letting it all wash over him. He trusted his subconscious pattern-recognition mind to let him know if something was off.

He got to the door of the low walk-up, its anachronistic style something that Dex had never seen in the physical world. He knew it was a fairly good historical reproduction from previous centuries, but as far as he knew there were none of those old buildings left. Progress had rendered them obsolete, left only to be remembered in images or vids — or recreated in M City.

He trudged up the stairs, enjoying the details — the cracks in the plaster and the grain in the wooden bannister. He was so focussed on the building that he nearly didn't notice that there was an unusual shadow cast on the frosted glass of his office door. He did notice, though, so was only slightly surprised to see Zahara Zhang sitting in his chair.

"Dex," she said as he opened the door. "Is everything all right in your neck of the woods?"

"Fine, Zizou, thanks for asking."

"There isn't a lot of information yet and we only see the highlights on our squad's boards." She seemed only to notice then that she was still in his chair and stood, but Dex waved her back down and sat in the visitor's chair across the desk.

"Nothing concrete yet," Dex said. "It still looks like it might just be an accident, even with everything else..."

Zhang nodded. "I know what you're talking about. I took a look beyond the highlights," she admitted, "and it's happening to you, too."

Dex was confused monetarily, then the penny dropped.

"You've been hit with the organized stuff."

"Yeah. I thought it was local to our squad. Honestly, I'd chalked it up to one particular bar manager who goes out of her way to piss people off. Her place was the source of half a dozen different petty incidents. It was easy to assume that she was the common link." Zhang shook her head. "I wonder how much useful time we wasted because I made that assumption."

Dex knew that feeling, and also knew it was pointless to dwell on past mistakes. "Any leads?"

Zhang shook her head. "It's the same story as you have here. None of the usual suspects have anything to do with it, the MOs are all across the board, but it's obviously targeted. It's like we're fighting shadows."

"It's almost like what went down in M City a few years back." Dex was just thinking out loud, but the look on Zahara Zhang's face made him listen to what he'd just said.

"What if it is?" she asked. "Then what?"

IT WAS THE KIND OF conversation that went down easier over a drink, so Dex and Zhang linked over to Monte's and found a quiet table in the back. Monte's was the local for Zhang's squad members, so she tended not to frequent the establishment — she always said that folks need a place to get away from their bosses. But it was the middle of the night in Namerica, so it was unlikely that they would run into anyone from the old team.

"Surely you didn't come all the way in here to check that I was okay?" Dex blew a plume of simulated smoke up into the dark rafters of the bar.

Zhang shook her head. "I was online anyway and your name popped up at shift start. I figured, why not just stop by? Old-fashioned style. I thought that would be up your street."

Dex laughed. His anachronistic tastes were well known. The smile faded from his lips as he said, "I'm sorry I don't have anything for you on your mystery inheritance. To be honest, I haven't even started."

"I didn't expect you would have," Zhang said. "I wanted to let you now that I've had another message from the legal team. That's what I was doing in M City — checking out my new property."

"And?"

She shrugged. "And, it's nothing to write home about. I mean, it's worth a fortune from my cop's salary perspective, and it's a perfectly functional data block. My... uh... tenants all seem completely legitimate. The only remarkable thing about it is that it's mine."

Dex nodded. "Did you find any hints as to why it is yours?"

"Like what? She didn't say anything in the will," Zhang said.

"Sure," Dex said, "but look at what she gave you." Zhang looked confused. "It's rez space. It's literally a communications medium, that's inherently locked down to the owner. If she'd wanted to leave you a message, she could have put it in the disk block itself."

Zhang's avatar froze for a moment. "I don't know if you're brilliant, or I'm an idiot," she said.

"Sir?"

"If I told you that I never ran a complete scan of the disk block, would you laugh?"

"No," Dex said. "But I would ask why not?"

"Well, to be honest I didn't really want to do anything that might come back to bite me if it transpired that the block wasn't legally Nightingale's to give."

"Fair enough. But, everything seems to be on the up and up?" Zhang nodded. "Well, then, maybe we should take a look and see if you've got anything hidden in there."

ZHANG HAD ACCESS TO every part of the block she owned, but she didn't want to go poking though the tenanted areas. "If there is a message for me in here, I can't imagine that Nightingale would have left it somewhere a tenant would find it."

Dex agreed and pored over the schematic Zhang brought up. The block was nearly fully leased, with one large rez space free.

"I did a walkthrough earlier," Zhang said, "I didn't see anything."

"Okay. Is there anywhere else that might be a good place for leaving a message to the new ownership? Some kind of equivalent of a maintenance room?"

They studied the schematic, and Zhang pointed at small area accessed off a hidden door. They linked over to a very small space that resembled a broom closet with some files and other documents in tight shelves.

"Oh, how clever," Zhang said, looking though the papers. "You can use these papers to set up tenancy and," she pulled out an interactive blueprint, "this looks like it lets you rerez the space. This is great, it's basically a visual representation of the admin interface."

Dex looked around at the shelves of documents and cleaning things. "What's this?" He held up a sealed envelope that felt like there was a hard, bulky item inside.

"Let's find out." Zhang tore open the envelope, and an old-fashioned looking device with a button fell out. She glanced at Dex who grinned back. She pressed the button.

A small holo image appeared in front of them — a generic avatar, female, with dark brown skin and a thoroughly nondescript face. It probably bore no resemblance to any actual human being on the planet but Dex was pretty sure it was meant to be Irina Nightingale.

"What a quaint way to leave a note," Zhang said as they waited for the avatar to deliver its message. It took longer to get going than seemed reasonable and when it became animated, Dex's hope for a quick solution disappeared.

The figure emitted a shrill noise that sounded like it had once been synthesized human speech but was now barely tolerable babble. The body jerked and convulsed, the sound and visuals completely unsynchronized.

"Are there any controls on that thing?" Dex asked as Zhang handled the small device.

"No, just this button." She pushed it and the keening sound ended as the holo abruptly disappeared. She hit it again, and the creepy broken file began to play from the beginning.

"Ugh, turn that thing off."

She did and chucked the device back into the envelope. "Well, that's annoying," she said. "A dead end."

"Damn it." Dex should have known it wouldn't be this easy, but he'd let himself get excited about an easy answer for once. Should have known better.

"SO, WHAT ARE YOU going to do with it?" he asked, after they'd linked back over to Monte's.

"Nothing, for the moment. It's not completely leased out, but there are several businesses and a couple of private instantiations hosted there. It's a good income. Like, quit your day job level good."

"Would you?" Dex asked after a minute.

Zhang shook her head. "I don't think so, anyway. It still doesn't seem real enough to make that kind of decision. Even now I'm about eighty percent confident you'll turn up something that makes it all go away. I mean, since when do people like us actually own property? It's ridiculous."

"Maybe," Dex said. "Or maybe it's the start of things changing around here."

Zhang laughed and downed the last of her cocktail. "Trust you to see the seeds of revolution in everything."

Dex started ticking points off on his fingers. "First, there's an international rash of organized petty crime that might be the prelude to some kind of massive turf war. Next, something that might be a bomb goes off. You think it's really all that strange to wonder if it's all connected? If there's something even bigger setting all this in motion?"

"No, I guess not," Zhang said, "but unlike you I'm not deathly allergic to coincidences. They do happen, Dex, like it or not. And some of this at least is almost certainly coincidence."

Dex snorted. "Your opinion is duly noted, Captain."

"Oh, Dex," Zhang said, her avatar's eyes sparkling with laughter, "don't ever change."

They clinked their glasses together and sipped in silence for a moment.

"I have, though," Dex said, quietly. "A lot."

"I know. And I'm happy for you."

"Thanks, Captain," Dex said. "I'm happy, too."

AFTER ZHANG LEFT, DEX linked back into his office. His feeds were all full of syndicated information from other squads. An industrial accident in Samerica was dominating the news — four people had been injured when scaffolding had failed at a Vertisales construction site. The chatter was trying to link it to the Nice explosion, but there was no real evidence to suggest a connection. The only similarities were the timing and how unusual both incidents were.

Dex didn't like it — didn't like anything that smacked of a coincidence. But he also didn't like the easy way people were drawing connections with no evidence. Making assumptions out of fear was no way to investigate anything. It was no way to live.

He knew he couldn't do anything about it, so tried to file it all away in a back compartment of his mind. He waded through the feeds to see if there was anything new in M City, anything specifically for his squad to do, but it was quiet.

"Too quiet," he said aloud to his empty office, then laughed at his own cliché. "Right. Time to make the doughnuts."

He pulled open the file on Zahara Zhang's mysterious benefactor and went through it all again. Irina Nightingale had owned a dozen data blocks in M City, which meant that she had controlled as much rez space as the network arm of one of the smaller firms. In the past few years, privately owned disk space was becoming more common, but the bulk of M City still ran on blocks supplied by the firms.

Networking was one of the few areas where the firms collaborated, but hosting space was a product like any other. Nightingale's holdings were just small enough to slide under the notice of the competing firms. She'd known her business.

Dex flipped through the simulated papers to see if there was any indication who had been bequeathed the other blocks. A copy of the relevant part of Nightingale's will had been included, but the section that referenced Zhang only covered three of the other blocks. And, of course, any identifying information about the other beneficiaries had been obfuscated. But details weren't necessarily the only way to get information.

The three other bequests that had been included in the file given to Zhang indicated that they were exactly the same as hers — a single data block, to a single individual. It was an assumption, but Dex guessed that the nine other data blocks would likely follow the same pattern, which meant that there were eleven other people out there who had just come into a windfall. And if he was lucky, that might make a traceable pattern.

Dex had no way of knowing who the other beneficiaries were. For all he knew, Zhang was the only one who didn't know Nightingale. She might be the only one who wasn't already a rez space mogul. But assuming that the other beneficiaries were equally ordinary, Dex figured that out of twelve people there had to be someone who was desperate for cash. Selling a whole block of disk space would be enough to let an average person quit their job, get private accommodation and live comfortably for quite some time. That had to be appealing.

He didn't know much about the disk business, but you could learn almost anything on the 'nets. And with the special backdoor access he had thanks to his squad work, anything that wasn't locked down by double crypto was available with a little digging. Dex sharpened his metaphorical shovel.

DEX HAD NEARLY BORED himself to death reading quarterly reports and the infinitely worse industry "news" magazine puff pieces on who was buying what. But eventually he stumbled upon a corporate blogger who kept a running tally of M City property sales. It was brain numbingly dull stuff, but exactly the mother lode Dex was hoping for. He scraped the feed and downloaded the data to his personal system. He'd get a script to look for anomalies, trying to identify anyone who might be one of the beneficiaries. He wondered if there might even be a way to use this data to identify Irina Nightingale, as well.

The legal papers Zhang had given him were sparse on useful details. There was the required affidavit from the legal team that Nightingale was the rightful owner of the goods being transferred and had the legal ability to make the bequest, but other than those assurances that it was all aboveboard, Nightingale could be anyone. The name could even be a pseudo or a multi. Dex wondered if the real Irina Nightingale was even dead.

He couldn't come up with a compelling reason that someone would create a fake persona, amass a small fortune, then kill off the persona and give away their estate, but it was theoretically possible. And he'd learned over the course of his time as an investigator, that if a thing was possible, someone would probably try it out sometime.

He was puzzling over the seemingly endless options when the phone on his virtual desk rang. Dex was still paging through feeds online, so he didn't bother losing focus from his onboard system to pick up the telephone handset. He just gave the thought command to his system, saw that it was Annabelle pinging him, and opened up a subvocal channel.

"Hi, kiddo, what's up?"

"I was just wondering the same thing."

Dex was puzzled for a moment, but she explained. "I've been home for an hour and you're still hiding out in the closet. Surely I haven't been rubbing off on you that much."

Dex laughed and linked out of M City. He found himself in his home "office" with a handful of food brick wrappers and an empty bottle of water. "I'll be out in a sec." He stood and caught a whiff of himself. "You might want to clear a path between me and the lav, though. I've been in here a while."

"You are such a sweet-talker, you." Dex could hear Annabelle's laughter through the closet door and in the small speaker implanted in his jaw. It was a funny sensation, but he loved it.

"I WOULDN'T WAGER MONEY on it, but if I were forced to give an opinion, I'd say it was an accident." René Biagini shrugged expansively and popped a small piece of real milk cheese in his mouth. It was an indulgence, but Biagini was never one to resist temptation.

"I saw the reports," Annabelle said from her seat in the corner. She'd given herself a wide buffer between herself and the rest of Le Rétro, but she seemed as at ease as she ever was in the physical world. "There might be some negligence involved, but I have to agree. Neither the fire nor the subsequent explosion appear to have been intentional."

Dex pursed his lips, making the other two laugh.

"You look like you ate something noxious," Biagini said.

"Coincidence," Dex said, "is something noxious."

Annabelle shrugged. "With all the people in the world, there are bound to be things that appear related but aren't. Surely it happens all the time."

"Of course," Dex said, "but usually they aren't anything important. They aren't anything unusual. And they almost never are both."

René and Annabelle shared a conspiratorial glance. "I never should have introduced the two of you," Dex said, with a faux grimace. "Two against one is grossly unfair."

René patted his hand and, in a deadpan, said, "Two against one is either a very lucky night indeed... or very expensive."

"Oh, René," Annabelle said, arching an eyebrow, "is that a proposition?"

"Don't encourage him," Dex said, trying to keep from smiling. It was an ongoing bit between the three of them — René's endless flirtation, Dex's mild embarrassment, Annabelle's enjoyment of both.

"Just a fact, mademoiselle," René said, leaning back and eating the last piece of cheese.

"Fun and games aside," Dex said, "I'll concede the point. The de Gaulle explosion was probably not part of this misdemeanour campaign. There hasn't been anything else like it reported by any of the squads and it just doesn't fit the pattern."

"What pattern?" Annabelle asked. "Seems to me it's been everything from petty vandalism to bullying. Why couldn't arson be included?"

"It's not the act that's outside the pattern," Biagini said, "it's the target."

"Or lack of a target," Dex finished. "All the other events seemed to be going after specific kinds of businesses — low value, high turnover, consumer shops. That's nothing like an industrial piece of infrastructure." He shrugged. "It looks very much like it is, after all, a coincidence."

Dex made a face and lifted a hand to catch the waiter's attention. He glanced at his companions to gauge their interest and saw two slight nods in return. He twirled a finger in the air to indicate another round and smiled at the waiter's acknowledgement.

"Just this one more," Biagini said. "I have an assignation later and do not wish to be late."

"I'm sure whoever it is would wait," Dex said, favouring his friend with a rare leer. "A little anticipation never hurt anyone."

René looked over at Annabelle, a look of mock outrage on his face. "Now who's the bad influence here, after all?"

"Oh, no. I'm not getting in the middle of you two," Annabelle said, then realized the double entendre. All three were still laughing when their drinks arrived.

ANNABELLE AND DEX WALKED back to the apartment hand-in-hand, the cool evening air raising gooseflesh on Dex's skin.

"I don't know, Dex," Annabelle said, "even if that mess at de Gaulle was just an accident, it really feels like things are getting worse."

"Yeah."

"It's not just low rent shops getting knocked over, either," she went on, "it's *everything*. I mean, working at Omnitrack used to be pretty good. Train schedules might be boring but optimizing them isn't — at least not for me." She chuckled. "But they used to pretty much leave me alone to get my work done. Now I have to actually go into the office, which is counter-productive on the face of it. I feel like I spend more time filling out timesheets than actually coding anything. And the things I'm working on..."

They walked another block, but Annabelle didn't finish her sentence. Dex knew that she was mulling something over. Pushing wouldn't help and she'd either finish her thought aloud or she wouldn't. Something was obviously bothering her, though. He kicked himself for not noticing — it couldn't have only come up today.

"This is obviously supposed to be on the QT," she said, dropping her voice. "My bosses haven't even admitted what we're doing. But come on, you'd have to be oblivious or totally unengaged not to see what we're being asked to do." She detangled her fingers from Dex's. She shoved her hands deep into her pockets and seemed to visibly shrink into herself. Dex recognized it as a calming technique and waited for her next move.

After a moment, she stopped walking and sat on a bench. Dex sat next to her, giving her a good half-metre. "You know how the firms used to more or less leave each other alone? Everyone had their own areas to operate in, at least for the big stuff?"

"Sure. Then a few years back, Omnitrack moved east in Namerica, into Aronson's territory. Now you're here in Europa. Some of the other big companies followed suit."

"Exactly. It's old-fashioned competition, good for everyone, right? Prices go down, more options, win-win."

Dex made a face. "It's not that simple. It hasn't been a win for you or your colleagues."

"That's my point," Annabelle said, looking miserable. "And it's going to get worse."

"What do you mean?"

Annabelle didn't say anything, but Dex felt a ping on his system. He went online and saw that Annabelle had created an encrypted chat. While it wasn't inconceivable that the public street they were on was equipped with a monitoring device, it seemed unlikely. Still, his own paranoia had come in handy on more than one occasion, so he logged into the chat.

"They've got me working on a double-whammy. Corporate espionage and sabotage."

Dex didn't know what to say. He knew he'd heard her correctly, but it couldn't be true. "That's... how can that even be happening?"

"Like I said, the jobs aren't labelled like that. And maybe I was being a bit unfair to my colleagues — it's not immediately obvious what we're doing. Collecting and analyzing Eurotrak's metadata is pretty clear, but it's also standard enough. And the other bit — well, maybe I'm just being irrationally suspicious. With all this shit going down out here..."

"There's nothing wrong with a little healthy suspicion. What's this 'other bit'?"

Annabelle sighed. "They say it's for internal systems testing. Basically, the equivalent of hiring a cracker to take a run at your systems to make sure they're tight. But I know our systems. The code they're getting us to write is not optimized for us. I'm pretty sure it's to crack into Eurotrak."

"Jesus, Annabelle."

"I know," she said, despair clear in her voice. "Saying it out loud like this... I can't keep doing it. So far they haven't asked me for anything that would be actually hazardous, but I can't know what they've given the other coders. And, of course, once they've got access, they could do anything. It's not just about what they want to do today, but what tomorrow's bosses decide to do."

Dex let out a long breath. "That's some heavy shit."

Annabelle's laugh startled him. "It is, at that," she said out loud, and ended the online chat. "Come on, you," she stood and held her hand out for him to take. "Let's go home. I've got some thinking to do."

WHEN THEY GOT BACK to the apartment, Dex left her alone with her thoughts. He knew what he thought she should do, but it wasn't his place to say it. Not now. If she asked him, that would be different, but for now she had to work through her own process.

Dex never really understood why she kept her corporate job in the first place. Her skills were heavily in demand in the freelance sector and she had the contacts to keep herself in as much work as she liked. She'd already given up her company apartment to move in with Dex — from his perspective there was less than nothing keeping her at Omnitrack even before the changes. But, as close as they'd become, Dex figured there would probably always be a few things about Annabelle he didn't understand. It went both ways — he still managed to surprise her on occasion. Most of the time, it was a good thing.

Dex got a bottle of bubbly water from the chiller and poured Annabelle a glass. He placed it on the small table next to her, knowing she could tell it was there even though her focus seemed to be entirely online. He grabbed a food brick and went into his closet office. He didn't bother closing the door, but with both of them at home and working online, it was the best way to give Annabelle some space.

He linked into his M City office out of habit rather than having a legitimate reason for being in the virtual world. He was only planning on looking at some files, which he could easily do on the heads-up screen overlay his implanted system provided. He'd grown accustomed to his office's interface, though, and the immersive nature helped him focus. He'd also never really liked that sense of seeing the physical world bleed through a screen.

His script had analyzed the data he'd gotten from the financial feeds and he settled in to check it out. It was still annoyingly dense and he had to fight to keep his attention on it. From what he could tell, when most data blocks technically changed ownership, they were really only being moved around internally between arms of the same corporation. There were a handful of private deals, but they were mainly sub-divided blocks — a private buyer taking full ownership of their rez space. Only two complete blocks had been listed for private sale in the past month, and only one since the Nightingale estate was settled. The seller was listed as S. Wu.

"Oh, for fuck's sake." How many S. Wus were there in the world? This was as bad as no name at all. Dex leaned back in his chair, closed his eyes and thought. What if he were a potential buyer? Surely there had to be a way to reach this particular S. Wu in order to make an offer.

He fired up the original feed where he'd found the listings and poked through the menus. Unfortunately, it wasn't a sales agency, just an individual with an odd set of interests, but Dex figured that someone this into virtual property markets would have the inside scoop on how one actually went about trading property.

He eventually found it — a listing of agencies which handled private sales. There were fewer than thirty. Dex could easily contact them all.

But to say what? He figured he could probably narrow down which agency was handling S. Wu's sale, but unless he could pony up the cash to buy the block, he was never going to get a whiff of the seller. The whole point of having a sales agent was so that the sellers didn't have to deal directly with the likes of him. And it's not like he could fake his way far enough into the sales process even if S. Wu did want to shake the hand of their buyer.

Dex linked out of M City and blinked a few times. It was dark and he'd neglected to put on the closet office's light. He had the lights come up low, then stood and stretched. He knew there was a simple solution. He probably would have thought of it regardless, but his conversation with Annabelle earlier brought it to mind immediately.

It wouldn't be difficult to break into the sales agents' files and simply take their client records. He wouldn't even need someone with Annabelle's skills — Dex was no programmer, but he had all kinds of dark ops scripts available to him. It wouldn't take long and he was sure he'd never get caught.

He'd done that kind of thing before. It didn't bother him, but this time he couldn't justify it. He'd have to come up with a more elegant solution before he resorted to breaking and entering. Just because he had the ability to get in and out without anyone noticing, that didn't mean he should use it. There had to be a line somewhere, even if it was arbitrarily drawn. Dex had long ago convinced himself it was the only thing that separated people like him from the people they chased, so he clung to that imaginary line as if it were the only thing between him and the abyss.

Sometimes, it was.

Seven

ANNABELLE HAD GONE TO WORK, after making it abundantly clear that she was not ready to talk about what she was going to do about the way her job had been changing. Dex knew not to push it, but he couldn't help feeling frustrated. For all her black hat skills, Annabelle was his ethical touchstone, and it was troubling to see her in a situation that was compromising. It wasn't his call, though, so he kept his mouth shut.

He hadn't magically come up with a solution to the S. Wu problem overnight, and a quick scan of his squad's bulletin didn't give him anything interesting to dig into. Given everything else going on, he couldn't get excited about the online equivalent of noise complaints. He swiped past the few outstanding items and marked himself as offline.

He shot a quick message to Biagini's team offering help. He knew it wasn't entirely within procedure, but he doubted anyone would mind. And he was fairly certain that an extra set of eyes wouldn't be turned away.

He wasn't wrong. He was getting dressed when his system pinged.

"I saw you've got some free cycles." It was Jamie Eristo. "I could use a hand on a burglary not far from you, if you're up for it."

Dex felt a familiar streak of excitement and noticed that it had been a while since he'd felt that way. "I'm up for it," he answered, a grin spreading across his face. "Send me the details and I'll meet you there."

DEX KNEW THAT IT was probably an indication that there was something not entirely right with him that he got excited about a burglary. But ever since he'd been assigned to the M City squad, he'd missed the stink and grime of handling cases in the physical world. He knew he was good at M City work — maybe it was his unique combination of being entrenched in the online community while not completely buying into it as a legitimate lifestyle. He was, as some religious people he'd once encountered described it, *in* the virtual world but not *of* the virtual world.

Whatever it was, Dex hadn't felt this energized by a job in a long time. He didn't even know what it entailed — it could be a boring, open and shut case — but as he walked along the Rue Liberté to the address Jamie had sent him, he was filled with a sense of anticipation.

A part of him wondered why that feeling didn't evaporate when he reached the small shop where Jamie was talking with a visibly angry woman. The shop was one of those hole-in-the-wall, "sell a little of everything" places that appear to be independently owned and operated, but are actually a branch of one or another of the major retail firms. This was a Techloid operation, based on the brands in the window. Or, former window, since it had been smashed.

Dex left Jamie to the irate shopkeeper, and examined the

shards of glass under the frame. Or, as it turned out, not glass — some kind of cheap polymer. Unlike Dex's old hometown in Namerica, many of the buildings in Nice still had some of the ancient architectural touches. Dumb glass, plaster walls, wood that actually came from a tree. This wasn't one of them, though. The window was a recent addition, made of the cheap but durable polymers favoured by most construction fabricators. So, how did these thieves break it?

Polymer glass wasn't indestructible by any means, but unlike old-fashioned glass, you couldn't just throw a rock through it. It took a specialized tool. And if you were the kind of thief who had a toolkit, surely you'd be able to pick the lock.

Dex caught Jamie's eye as he made his way over to the shop's door. The woman was still going on about the inconvenience — obviously an employee. Dex gave her an understanding smile and slipped into the shop, while Jamie explained his presence.

"This is a colleague of mine," they said.

"Oh, great!" the employee said, sighing dramatically. "Just what I need. More people stomping through here, making even more of a mess. If we aren't open for trading, I don't get paid, but no one else is going to clean this up. Or, is that what your colleague is here to do, eh?"

Dex shot Jamie a sympathetic look, but didn't stick around to help. He confirmed his suspicion that the lock hadn't been damaged. It wasn't that great a model, so someone with the right tools could have opened it without leaving a trace, but given the state of the window, that didn't seem likely. Dex scanned the shop and felt a pang of sympathy for the woman haranguing Jamie. It was a disaster in there.

Boxes and bags were strewn about the floor, more than a few of which had been slashed open, their contents dumped everywhere. Something liquid had been added to the mix making a slurry of who-knows-what on the floor. There was a discernible trail of destruction leading from the window, to the main shop aisle, to the chiller, then back toward the door. It was going to be a real challenge just to figure out what they took. Dex guessed that head office wouldn't even bother discerning between what was stolen and what was destroyed — it was all spillage either way.

Dex stopped and looked around the shop. It was a mess, certainly, and much of the inventory had been wrecked. But there was still plenty of stock on the shelves, and the two smaller aisles looked like they hadn't even been touched. Roughly comparing the empty shelves and the mess on the floor, Dex wondered if the robbers had even taken anything.

Which would mean that *robbers* wasn't entirely accurate — *vandals* was the better term. And if it was vandals, they certainly went to a lot of trouble. Waiting until the store was closed, bringing a special glass breaker. If they'd just wanted to wreck up the joint, they could have walked in at any time, wreaked their havoc and run away.

The employee appeared to have run out of steam, because Jamie joined Dex in the store.

"This is some mess," they said, prodding a pile of ShrimpySnax bags with a toe. "I get why Liisa's pissed." Jamie jerked their head toward the door, where the employee was leaning against the wall, staring into the middle distance. Online.

"Any chance this is about her?" Dex asked. Jamie frowned and Dex explained. "I'm not convinced that whoever did this was after goods. There's plenty of decent stuff still here, and this is probably more of a problem for her personally than anything else."

"You think it could be a personal revenge thing?" Jamie asked. "That would make more sense than anything else, but you saw the window, right?" Dex nodded. "That was a pro job. Or at least, it's not a civilian job. Whoever did this had to have access to a glass breaker."

"Construction?"

Jamie shrugged. "Could be, I suppose." They ran a hand over their short cropped hair and sighed. "I guess I'm going to have to talk to Liisa some more."

"I can take it, if you want? Sort of a good cop... other, different-but-also-good cop kind of thing?"

Jamie barked a short laugh and nodded. "Thanks. I'll get what I need from the scene." They closed their eyes for a moment. "And thanks again for helping out. It's been..." They took a breath and let it out slowly, as if performing a mediation or an anxiety-reduction technique. "It's been busy. This is the third incident I've been to today."

Dex actually checked the time on his display. "When did your day start, midnight?"

Jamie shook their head. "Thankfully, no. But the morning has been pretty full on. It was all starting to swim together if you know what I mean."

"Sure thing," Dex said. "You get your CSI on and I'll talk to..."

"Liisa."

"Got it." Dex gave Jamie's shoulder a squeeze, and turned to head out the door. Good cop. Other, different-but-also-good cop. No problem.

"SO, NOW THIS IS MY FAULT?!"

"That's not what I'm saying at all." Dex was using his best "make the other person comfortable" voice, but it didn't seem to make a difference. Liisa was already angry and any little thing which could contribute to that feeling was going to set it off. And Dex had set it off with a bang.

"Oh, really? Do I know of anyone who might have a grudge against me, who might decide that trashing the store is a good way of getting back at me? How is that not my fault?"

"Well—" Dex started, but Liisa wan't done yet.

"What do you think is going to happen if this comes back on me? You think my boss is going to say, 'Well, you couldn't know that some jerk-off you turned down in a date room would trash your workplace to get back at you, so we'll just pay you overtime for cleaning it all up, oh and here's a promotion for your trouble.'? Not fucking likely, is it? No, the much more likely scenario is that I'll get fired. If I'm really lucky, they won't dock the cost of the lost inventory from my last pay. So, you really think I'd tell you if I thought someone was doing this to completely fuck me over? Because that's exactly what this has done, by the way."

She ran out of steam, but Dex didn't have a good response. She was probably right about everything she'd said. He'd heard of worse things happening to employees after a break-in. Retail staff were easy to come by; there was no incentive for an employer to take a chance on someone who might be bringing trouble, however inadvertently.

"Look," he said, finally, "I get it. And I'm not going to make you put yourself in a bad position. But I don't work for your boss." He looked into the shop toward where Jamie was taking a video. "Neither of us do. This is a Techloid shop, right?" Liisa nodded. "They might send their own security, eventually. It probably depends on the loss amount, that's usually how it works. Anyway, they'll do their own investigation, and you'd be right to keep your mouth shut if you think it's someone who is out for you. But if you do think you know who it is, and you want something done about that..."

Dex gave her a serious look and he could see the message getting across. All the anger seemed to flow out of Liisa's body, and it looked like it was all that had been keeping her going. She slumped against the wall and Dex wondered if she was going to stay upright.

She did, if only barely. "Sorry I've been such an asshole."

"It's okay," Dex said, then glanced into the shop. "It's a shit show in there."

That made her laugh, but it died out quickly. "I'm going to be cleaning it up for hours. But I can't afford to get fired, so..." She shrugged. "Look, I honestly don't know of anyone who'd do this to me. I really don't think that's what this is, but who knows, right? I— if I hear about anything, I'll let you know, okay?"

Dex nodded. If this was a revenge play, whoever it was would probably want to get a gloat in. He had to admit that it was the most likely way they'd find out who did it. Otherwise, these kinds of cases remained unsolved more often than not.

Jamie joined them out in front of the shop. "I've got everything I can get," they said. "And you?"

Dex shook his head. "Liisa's going to let us know if anyone gets in touch, but it's a long shot."

"If you're done, I've got to get started on that," Liisa said, looking forlornly at the mess in the shop.

"Go ahead," Jamie said. "You've got something to cover

the open window?"

"Yeah, there's spare polyglass in the back. It's just another thing on my list." She sighed and trudged into the store, the door sliding closed behind her.

EIGHT

"WHAT KIND OF PERSON DOES THAT?" Jamie asked as they walked with Dex toward the train station. "Trashing things for the fun of it? Don't they realize that some poor soul has to deal with it?"

"Well, if that's the point of it..."

"You really think it was targeted at her?"

Dex shrugged. "She wasn't exactly forthcoming with potential suspects, but no one wants to admit they pissed someone off enough to make them come back with glass breakers and buddies..." He broke off, thinking. "Hey, did that look like a multiple person job to you?"

Jamie nodded. "I got at least two sets of footprints off the crap on the floor," they said. "Why?"

"Well, unless Liisa's a lot more interesting than she seems, I can't see her getting a group riled up enough to pull this off. I wonder if I've been barking up the wrong tree."

"If you've been *what*?"

"Sorry," Dex laughed. "It's an old expression. Means going down the wrong path."

"Well, it's not really your path to go down," Jamie said as

they approached the train station, "but I do appreciate the help. You know, you weren't too bad on the real streets, Mister Virtual Detective. We could use someone like you about now."

"Don't tempt me, kid," Dex said. "Now go file your report, before I make a rash decision."

Jamie smiled and turned into the train station. Dex watched them go, thinking that it had been a bit of lighthearted banter, but Jamie was right. He had missed working cases out here and he was good at it. There was something about pounding feet on a solid, dirty, real street. And it was true that the squad probably could use another set of feet on the street.

The temptation was real.

DEX'S SYSTEM PINGED A couple of times on his way home, but it was just the M City squad. Nothing was labeled as urgent, so he swiped them away; he wanted to stay in the physical world a little longer. He took the long way home, through the Pietonne. The wide boulevard with trees, public art and benches still struck him as the kind of fantasy most people escaped to Marionette City to enjoy.

For over six decades Dex had lived in a highly functional if colourless city, where changing neighbourhoods was an exercise in exchanging one version of grey, utilitarian buildings for another. But most of Europa was different; cities and towns here retained at least a flavour of their heritage. The inhabitants of Nice, in particular, had fought to keep as many of their historical buildings and public spaces as possible.

Sure, there were plenty of industrial complexes and high-rise corporate apartment blocks, but there was also more. There was a feeling of humanity here that Dex had never even known he was missing. Moving here had been like coming home, as much as that made no rational sense. That Annabelle lived here had been no small part of it, of course, but when he'd told her he wasn't moving for only her, he'd been telling the truth. It was like living in a world of black and white, then waking up one morning to 128-bit colour.

Dex breathed deeply, the scent of the trees mingling with a deeper, loamier smell. The warm breeze off the Mediterranean brought a sweet salt tang, with an undercurrent of what he now thought of as "low-tide" smell. The scent of the coast rarely reached as far inland as his apartment, but it was only a thirty-minute walk to the Promenade. He vowed to put the effort in to get there more often. What was the point of living somewhere if you didn't take advantage of its perks?

Not today, though. He turned north instead of south, heading back to his apartment. He'd spent the whole morning helping Jamie and little fingers of guilt were kneading the back of his mind. In an eerie confluence of timing, his system pinged again. This time it was Mack Larsen himself, on a person-to-person line. Dex kept walking, but subvocally answered the call.

"I'm glad I got though." Larsen's gruff voice was laced with what sounded like genuine concern. "After the explosion, I was wondering if things have kicked off over there and we just hadn't heard anything."

Dex looked around at the people out in the warm afternoon, walking, laughing, sharing meals. A songbird trilled peacefully from a nearby power line. It was about as far away from "kicking off" as he could imagine.

"No, everything is fine here," Dex said, tamping down the ever-increasing feeling of being caught in the middle of something. "A rash of minor street crime, but I understand that's not confined to this jurisdiction."

"And the bomb?"

"It wasn't a bomb," Dex said, "at least there's no evidence of that. From what I hear, the official word is accident, but they're still looking into it."

"So you don't think it's related?" Larsen asked, his voice taking on a sharper tone. "This isn't some major issue we all need to get in front of?"

"Don't think so, sir."

"Well then, Mister Dexter, can you explain why you have been unreachable for the past twenty-four hours, when this roster I have here shows quite clearly that you are scheduled to be on duty?"

Oh, shit. The little fingers of guilt curled themselves into a fist.

"Not really, sir," Dex said. "It seemed more important to be helping with the situation out here. But..." He knew the guilty feeling was his own subconscious telling him that he'd fucked up. It was time to own up to it. "But it probably wasn't."

Larsen sighed. "The thing is, whether it was or wasn't a better use of your time isn't the issue. It's not your call. Yes, our organization is decentralized and yes, we all have a lot of individual latitude. We aren't a corporate security department. But we are an organization. We have squads and divisions and assignments for a reason and as much as you might like to think so, it's not so people like me can get high on the power. It's so that the people we serve all get a fair shot. That's the reason this whole business began, Dex, you know that. To give everyday people who didn't have access to some firm's security a chance at something that looks like justice. And it's no less unfair when you're the one deciding what cases do and don't matter than it is when it's the head office of Gractor or Monitech. Am I making myself clear, Detective?"

Christ almighty, Dex hated Mack Larsen. And it was much, much worse when the man was right.

"Crystal, sir," Dex answered. "And thanks for the reminder."

DEX FELT LIKE A HEEL. He was glad that Annabelle was still at work when he got to the apartment. He took a quick shower, ate a food brick, then silently berated himself for putting off the inevitable.

He got some supplies — a bottle of water, some crunchy snack food supplements Annabelle had gotten him hooked on — and settled himself into the chair in his office. Time to pay the piper.

He logged into M City and linked straight into the vestibule of the office block in Kanzai district where Mack Larsen's squad was based. Dex rarely showed his face in the office, a perk of his position. But today he marched his avatar past the receptionist who gave him a cordial nod, and walked into the squad room.

There were only two other avatars in the space. Dex recognized Hitori Sommerdale poring over a colourful chart, but he had to bring up an identity overlay to get the name of the other person. A translucent tag hovered over the head of the tall, dark-skinned female-presenting avatar paging rapidly through a vid file — Ruby Magoro. Dex recognized her name from the reports, but he'd never seen her avatar before. That was pretty terrible. What kind of a teammate was he? How many of the squad had he never even met?

They both obviously knew who he was, though, because once his presence was known they both looked up and greeted him by name.

"What brings you here?" Sommerdale asked, no hint of malice in his voice. Dex figured that Larsen had kept his rebuke private. Typical. Dex didn't even have the luxury of being able to sensibly apologize to these folks.

"I've got a bit of downtime," Dex said, "wondered if you could use another set of eyes on anything."

The other two avatars froze for a brief moment, and Dex was fairly certain they were exchanging a few side-channel words. It didn't last long, though, and Magoro said, "That would be great."

She showed Dex the video she was analyzing, explaining that one of the independent tea shops in the Borderlands district was having repeated attempts to disrupt its rez code. "They haven't had a problem yet," she explained, "the automated counter-measures are working fine. But it keeps happening and we're trying to see if we can figure out the source."

"You think it's a specific attack on the shop?" Dex asked, thinking of the busted up storefront he'd walked though earlier that day in Nice.

"You'd think so, because it's a repeat attack," Sommerdale said without looking up from his chart, "but to what end? If it were actually doing some damage, I could see it. But their system catches the incursion before it can have any impact on the rez itself, so it's almost a case of no harm no foul."

"Why are you— uh, why are *we* involved, then?"

"Preventative measures," Sommerdale said.

"And curiosity," Magoro added. "Like, if you're specifically trying to mess up this tea house, surely you'd quit wasting your resources on an attack that doesn't do anything? But what if it's just a test case? Or an error? Or—"

"You can see why another viewpoint on this might be helpful," Sommerdale interrupted with a chuckle. "Ruby and I have gone around in circles on this one."

"Well, I'm happy to take a look," Dex said. "I'm no great shakes with code, but I'll do what I can." He walked over to a desk and asked if it was free.

"Sure," Magoro said, "just don't move anything around. Susana likes everything to be tickety-boo."

"Gotcha," Dex said, wishing he'd picked a desk other than the one used by Susana Bells, the second-in-command. But he wasn't about to waste more time worrying about where his incorporeal form was pretending to be. And it wasn't as if Dex using the desk prevented anyone else from using it — it was a virtual construction that could exist in as many versions as was required. People tended to interact in M City as if it were a one-to-one analogue of the physical world, but of course it wasn't.

Dex grabbed copies of the files Sommerdale and Magoro were working on, and they appeared to materialize on the desk in front of him. He understood why they had gotten sucked in by this case. It didn't seem to have any significant repercussions, but it was a puzzle.

Just like Zahara Zhang's mysterious benefactor was a puzzle. And why an otherwise perfectly good power store would catch fire was a puzzle. And who knocked over the

Techloid shop was a puzzle.

Puzzles were addictive and like many drugs, giving up one often meant taking up another. It might not be his first choice, but Dex could get his fix with this puzzle for a while. He settled in and started to read over the files.

Nine

DEX WAS STILL LOGGED INTO the M City squad room when he heard Annabelle come home. He made sure that he left Susana's desk as he'd found it, said goodbye to Magoro who was still there, and linked out.

He opened the door to the closet/office, making sure to make some noise so as not to startle Annabelle. She was by the chiller, peering inside.

"Rough day?" he asked.

Annabelle made a sound somewhere between sigh and a groan. Under other circumstances, it was the kind of noise that might have sent a wave of heat throughout Dex's body, but this was not a sound of pleasure.

"Anything I can do?"

"Buy a girl a drink?" Annabelle said, closing the chiller drawer with a loud *snick*.

Dex grinned. "That is a thing within my capabilities. So, options: I can run down the street for a bottle of synthwine, we could head over to Le Rétro, or link over to Montes." He ticked off the suggestions on his fingers, then held up his hand. Annabelle smiled and grabbed his ring finger, giving it a slight squeeze.

That warm feeling began to swim inside Dex's body after all.

ANNABELLE WAS WEARING HER drab one-piece Omnitrack uniform in Nice, but in M City she wore slim trousers and a gauzy, thin top with a shimmer of colour that subtly changed every time Dex looked at it. He wore his usual charcoal pinstripe suit, but instead of the gaudy bright red tie he often chose, he'd opted for an open-collar black shirt and an emerald pocket square.

Annabelle's eyes grew large. "You've been shopping. Should I be worried?"

Dex laughed. At one time, that question might have been serious, but it had been a long time. Dex didn't really know what an old married couple should act like, but he guessed that the two of them fit the bill.

"I had a case at a haberdashery last month," Dex explained, "and it dawned on me that I hadn't changed this —" he gestured at his avatar's body, "in a good long while. So, I picked up a couple of things. Like what you see?" A smile tugged at the corners of his lips.

Annabelle held a serious expression on her face as she inspected him from several angles. Then, she reached over and carefully undid another button on his shirt, letting her finger rest on the divot under his Adam's apple for about a hundred years.

Since he'd upgraded his implants, the sensation of things in Marionette City was unnervingly similar to their physical analogues. It wasn't the same, but Dex had slowly gotten over the general feeling of wrongness that came from the subtle difference. As Annabelle's avatar touched his, and his implants did their simulated magic, the breath in his physical body caught.

"Mm-hmm," Annabelle said, finally drawing away. "Green suits you."

Dex had no idea what she was talking about for a moment, then the conversation came back to him, along with his ability to speak. "Glad you like it. Drink?"

"Definitely."

They ordered from the menu interface, Annabelle taking her time selecting. She'd be ordering stims with her virtual drink, so that when her avatar took a sip, her implants would direct an analogous amount of whatever stim she chose to her brain. It was no different than using a stim cartridge, but it all happened through the M City interface. Technology was grand.

Dex stuck to a flavour-only drink, which he sipped as Annabelle took a deep draught of her neon blue concoction. She closed her eyes and let out a deep breath. Dex could hear her physical body making the same movements next to him.

"Oh, I needed that," Annabelle said, opening her eyes.

"Things are getting worse?"

She shook her head, then shrugged. "I don't know. I'm starting to think that if it's not better it's worse, you know? The more this goes on the more I don't think I can do it anymore. But what else am I going to do?"

"You have a lot of options, kiddo," Dex said softly.

He expected an argument, but Annabelle didn't say anything for a moment. Finally, she reluctantly agreed.

"I guess I've spent so long just assuming that I'd always have a corp job that I never seriously considered going out on my own. It just never felt like a real possibility, so I never thought about it."

Dex nodded. He'd wanted Annabelle to go independent long ago; she was infinitely more qualified than he was, after all. But it wasn't his decision and he didn't want his opinion to influence the decision she did make.

"What about another company? Omnitrack isn't the only game in town, after all."

Annabelle shook her head. "I thought about it, looked around a little. The truth is I don't see anyone else with a better offer. The opposite, actually." She took another pull on her drink, then set down the glass. She turned it on the table absent-mindedly and chewed her bottom lip. It wasn't common for an avatar to display unconscious behaviour, but a few people had the necessary interface upgrades to allow it. Dex had to agree that it did add nuance to online interactions that made them much richer.

"I made a few discreet enquiries," Annabelle said, "and had a couple of offers. One was pretty serious. But it was obvious that they both wanted me more for whatever information about Omnitrack I could bring, rather than my actual skills."

"You never mentioned this," Dex said, then immediately wished he hadn't. Or at least, that he'd managed to keep the accusatory tone out of his voice. "I'm sorry. You don't have to tell me every little thing that goes on in your day. I'm not your boss."

"It's okay." Annabelle reached out to take Dex's hand. "I didn't mention it because it felt... disloyal, maybe?"

"Not disloyal to me?"

"No," Annabelle laughed, "to Omni, I guess?"

"Why would I care about you being loyal to Omnitrack?"

Annabelle squeezed his hand. "It's not about you, sweetie."

Jesus. He was doing it again. What was wrong with him? "I know, I'm sorry."

"I guess I thought if I told you, that would make it real, make it important. And I really didn't think I was serious about leaving Omnitrack. Certainly, the responses I got didn't encourage me to pursue it any further. But now..." She pulled away and stared off into the distance, as if looking for an answer in the unrezzed edges of Three Card Monte's bar.

"I don't think I can stay there," she said, finally. "This is hard. I know what I am. I've written plenty of malicious, invasive and low down unethical packages. But I've tried to use them for good reasons. Maybe the reasons don't matter, and maybe Omni is just asking me to do the same thing for them that I've done for you or Mack Larsen or Captain Zhang. But it doesn't feel the same to me. I'm a cracker; I have no business trying to take the ethical high road. But I can't keep doing what they're asking me to do."

Dex thought about the things he had done, things which if they were publicly known would get him in the bad books of more security departments than he'd had hot meals. Things which, if someone did them to him or someone he loved, he'd be none too pleased. But he believed, in his bones, that his work was making things better. Whenever he threatened some would-be shake-down artist, he felt like he was on the side of the angels. Back in the day, when things got physical, that never bothered him, either. In a perfect world, everyone would treat each other with respect, but this was far from a perfect world, and sometimes you had to operate from the edges.

But now wasn't the time to convince Annabelle that

morally grey was good enough.

"Okay, then," Dex said. "Sounds like you've made a decision. What's the plan?"

WHEN THEY FINALLY LINKED out of M City, Dex was hungry and thirsty and tired. He put together a quick meal of a liquid nutritional supplement Annabelle liked and they sat together at the table to eat.

"Now that I've actually made a decision, I feel like I have to go in tomorrow and give my notice," Annabelle said.

"Given the project you've been working on, you think they'll be happy to let you go?"

"Probably not," Annabelle said, "but what are they going to do? I mean, I'm sure I'll be escorted out of the building and all my accesses revoked immediately."

"Maybe I'm being paranoid," Dex said, "but if it were me, I'd have you followed for a while, too."

"Ugh. You're probably right."

"Can you stick it out a little longer?" Dex asked. "Enough time to at least have a few conversations, line up something else? We're fine for euros for now, but if Omni are going make life difficult, it would be good to have your ducks in a row before you quit."

Annabelle nodded. "You're right. I just feel like I've already left, you know? And the longer I stay, and the more this project goes on, the more incriminating information I'll have access to. That's the thing that really worries me — that they'll guess that I've figured out what's going on and decide that I'm selling them out to one of their competitors."

Dex nodded. "All the more reason to get something else

in the works, something that has nothing to do with trains. They might not buy it, but at least then you'll have something to sell them."

"You're a smart cookie, Andersson Dexter," Annabelle said. "I'm glad you're on my team."

"Always, kiddo."

"So, do you have any brilliant ideas for getting freelance work? Do you think Larsen has budget for a full-time cracker on the squad?"

Dex thought back to his afternoon helping out Sommerdale and Magoro. He'd been useful enough, but he couldn't pretend that the squad was swamped, and he was the only member of the team that wasn't a code jockey of some sort. He made a face.

"I don't think so. He'd have mentioned it to you if he did."

Annabelle frowned. "Yeah, he hasn't called me in for a while. I guess that would have been too easy."

"Well," Dex said, "there is someone who has been wanting to get you on the payroll for a while now."

Annabelle looked genuinely confused.

"Have you seriously forgotten?" he asked.

"Forgotten what?"

"Stella Bish."

Even saying the name made Dex feel awkward. Bish was, among other things, their landlord, owning the entire La Liberté complex. She ran a freelancer empire based in M City and in acquiring the residence she saw an opportunity that both helped the people who worked with her and was a lucrative investment. That was the contradiction that Bish embodied — ruthless at business but always in the middle of projects that made life better for ordinary people. Until he'd met her, Dex had always assumed those two goals were at odds, but Bish managed to be both entirely mercenary and socially responsible. It was unnerving.

"What are you talking about?" Annabelle asked. "I doubt she even knows who I am."

"What are *you* talking about?" Dex countered. "After the way you helped her when her online accounts were being compromised? And everything that you did with the crypto package for M City? She knows who you are, all right, and she wants you on her team."

"How do you know that? Do the two of you have regular conversations now?"

Dex shook his head and visibly shuddered. "Thankfully, we do not. You know she gives me the creeps. I haven't talked to her since she turned up at Monte's that time. After that "Mission" business, remember? When she offered you a position? Said that you should call her first if you ever wanted to go independent? Gave you her card?"

"Oh. That."

"Yeah," Dex said, "that."

 Ten

DEX SEEMED TO HAVE gotten back into Mack Larsen's good graces after spending several days at the Kanzai office. He ran into the man's huge avatar in the hallway and Larsen clapped him on the shoulder.

"Good work on the tea shop business."

"Thanks, sir," Dex said, "but Magoro cracked it. All I really did was give her someone new to talk to."

Larsen shook his head. "It's teamwork, Dex. Good to see." The wide smile on his face faded. "Not so great to see that the consortium is up to its old tricks."

"More likely they never stopped," Dex said. "Annabelle tells me that until everyone in M City is running the counter-incursion code, they'll keep looking for ways to take over. She says they're probably using automated scripts — it's theoretically possible that the people behind it originally aren't even involved anymore. It's just ticking over like a windup toy."

"A bot," Larsen said.

Dex nodded. "But, I bet there's still someone running the show. The firms can't be happy that we're carving out a shadow world in here that they can't control."

"No," Larsen said, "I'm sure they aren't. Anyway, good work. I'm glad to see you're back on board."

Dex's physical body flushed with a combination of guilt, embarrassment and annoyance. His avatar betrayed nothing, though.

Larsen gave him the once over, then said, "I know you hate it here."

"Sir?"

Larsen twirled a finger in the air. "This office. It's not your style, not your style at all." He grinned. "I don't want to be some form-filling middle management flunky. If you'd rather work out of that rat-trap in Chandlers or log in using some godforsaken command line interface, I don't care. I'm not going to make you turn up here just to be seen. We're all adults, right?"

"Sir."

"Just keep me in the loop if you're going to be offline for a while, all right?"

"Yes, Captain."

"Okay, get out of here. I can tell that all this glass and chrome is about to give you hives."

Larsen turned to head down the hall and Dex shook his head. The captain was maddening and so strange, but he wasn't wrong. Dex linked over to his private office before Larsen had even reached his own door.

HE FINISHED THE LAST of his reports, pulling a virtual sheet of paper out of the typewriter on his scarred, wooden desk. He collected all the sheets, marked them for filing, then slid them into the tray marked "Out" on the edge of his desk. His system uploaded the text to the appropriate case files but to Dex's avatar's eyes, the papers disappeared in a small cloud of sparkles. It was cheesy but effective, and always added to his sense of accomplishment at the end of the day.

The usual sense of finality didn't settle over him, though. He opened his whiskey drawer and poured a short shot. He lit a cigarette and sipped, then pulled the manila file containing his notes on Zahara Zhang's inheritance. After his conversations with Annabelle, he had ethics on the mind, and was even more reluctant to try to get information about S. Wu the easy way. But he hadn't figured out what the hard way even was.

He flipped through the papers, hoping something he'd overlooked would jump out at him. On a whim, he ran a search for the name in the M City database. It didn't take long for his system to come back with a uselessly high number. Well, at least he was right about that. He downed his shot to celebrate the empty victory.

He was about to call it a day when he got an idea. He'd been trying to find the person selling the block of disk space, but maybe he should be looking at the space itself. He dug through the listings to see if the agent was offering virtual tours. It took a bit of deciphering the sales language but eventually Dex figured out how to set up a time to have a viewing. They didn't require a down payment for that, at least.

He wasn't sure what he could learn by looking at some random instantiations, but it was something to do. And sometimes just getting started was all it took for things to begin to come together.

HE SHOULD HAVE KNOWN that the sales agents would have an automated system for showing properties. It was one of the distinct advantages of doing business in M City — simple tasks could be staffed with bots rather than people. Most sales staff in shops were bots, ditto for receptionists, waiters, anything that didn't require a real time complex communication. Showing off some disk space was a perfect bot job.

Dex linked to the public portal near the block that S. Wu was selling, in a profoundly ordinary section of Quayside. It was a nice district of M City, modelled after a seaside town, with several areas devoted to al fresco cafés, public spaces and recreational facilities. Wu's disk block, however, had no natural view and was filled with a nondescript array of tenants. There were two avatar customization shops, a large portfolio space that appeared to belong to a cooperative of several designers, a dingy-looking office building and a flashy sex bot outlet. All in all, it could be any random block in M City.

The sales bot found Dex with no difficulty and made a canned introduction. The bot was wearing a high femme avatar and Dex wondered if the agency customized their staff according to whoever was making enquiries. He hadn't given them much to go on, so he figured this was the standard. Perhaps if he came back for a second look, they'd put little more effort in.

"Thank you for your interest in this block, Mr. Dexter," the bot said in a breathy voice. "I can take you into the public areas of course, and you can see the outside of the rez space easily enough. Are you interested in a leasing investment opportunity? The tenants of this space have all been here for quite some time and are very happy to stay on. Once your interest has been registered properly, with a small deposit, we can provide you with the financials — lease payments, liens, any other information you might require to make a decision."

Did this bot ever stop talking?

"Please show me whatever you can," he said in the hopes that it would trigger the next part of the bot's program. Thankfully, the bot turned and led Dex into the sex shop first. The space was nice enough — high ceilings, plenty of back room storage. There was nothing wrong with it that Dex could see. The shop was also staffed by a bot, and Dex recognized the models on display as Odyssey brand units. He couldn't remember which firm made the Odysseys, but they were reasonable quality, mass market items.

The virtual estate bot then led Dex methodically through the other shops, which were all similar in layout. She explained that the office space was sub-leased to individuals who were able to use it for whatever instantiation they wished. "This area is zoned for mixed use, so there is a good diversity among the tenants here." Dex wondered about how well this bot was programmed, given that there was really no such thing as zoning in M City. The different districts each had their own aesthetic, which external rezzes were expected to maintain, but there was no way to control what people did with their internal instantiations. And no reason to care.

After the tour, Dex thanked the bot and suffered through a painful spiel designed to make him think that a) this disk space was unique in vague and unprovable ways, b) that it was a nearly criminal bargain, and c) that it was bound to be snapped up by a canny investor Any Minute Now. It wasn't quite the hard sell, but he didn't expect more subtlety from this construct. He escaped as soon as he could.

DEX COMPILED ALL THE information he'd gotten from the viewing, but it wasn't much. He took a few shots of the external space and had a list of the tenants that the sales bot gave him. It felt a bit like a waste of time, but he didn't have a lot of other ideas. He folded it all into a quick report and sent it off to Zahara Zhang, asking if there was anything that looked familiar. Hoping for a random connection was weak, but Dex was willing to try anything. It also let Zhang know that he hadn't forgotten about her.

He paged over to the squad board to make sure he wasn't ignoring something. He didn't particularly want to get another tongue lashing from Larsen. All the open cases had been claimed by someone and there wasn't anything that cried out to him as requiring his particular talents. He figured that he could let it slide for now.

He switched over to the Nice squad's board, and checked to see if Jamie had made any headway on the shop. There weren't any leads, but they had noted that Techloid had determined that Liisa hadn't had any responsibility for the incident and she had kept her job. Dex wondered how much unpaid overtime she'd put in cleaning up the mess and whether it had been worth it. He remembered his own days working shit jobs, not having any other options. No job meant no apartment, no food rations, no security, nowhere to turn.

That some people were now able to make a living in M City, on their own, meant that the firms' control over people's lives was diminishing. But it was easy to forget that it was only a small proportion of people who had gotten out from that trap. People like Liisa were the norm, and they were at the mercy of the vagaries of their HR department. With the firms now actively trying to sabotage each other, both in M City and in the physical world, the real casualties were going to be people like her.

It sucked, but what could you do about it?

Dex linked out of M City and rubbed his hands over his tired eyes. He managed to go days without thinking about how shitty life was for so many people, but it always came crashing back eventually. He knew that he was doing his small bit to make things better, but it didn't feel like it was ever enough.

He stomped around the apartment in a foul mood, glad that Annabelle was out. She'd been talking to Stella Bish and was in the process of getting everything in order to leave Omnitrack, but she was still going into the office. Dex wasn't sure how they were going to handle being in the same space all day every day. Given Annabelle's discomfort with the physical world, it was incredible that she managed the time together they did share. He wondered if she realized that this was probably one of the reasons she stuck with a corporate job all this time.

Something was niggling at the back of Dex's mind. It was like he could tell that there was a pattern, just waiting to be found, but he wasn't seeing it yet. It was there, he knew it, just out of focus or overly pixellated.

He grabbed a bottle of expensive ginger beer that one of his neighbours brewed at home, and splashed a hint of it into a glass of rum. He hadn't done anything to earn the treat, but maybe it would jog his mind into seeing whatever it was that was just outside of the frame. He took a sip and waited for the elixir to work its magic.

Nothing happened, except the enjoyment of the drink.

Well, worse things have happened than having a cheeky highball alone, standing in the middle of an empty apartment.

ELEVEN

RENÉ BIAGINI LIFTED HIS GLASS HIGH and said, loudly enough for the entire street to hear, "Here's to the latest arrival at Emancipation Station!" Glasses clinked, hoorays were cheered and Dex stole a glance at Annabelle to make sure she wasn't too freaked out by all the people. She seemed to be holding her own, so he leaned over.

"Emancipation Station? What is he going on about?"

"Beats me," she said. "René stopped making sense about... three rounds ago."

She had been right about what she thought would happen when she gave her notice. That afternoon she'd been escorted out of the Omnitrack building by two burly security officers, who had waited outside their apartment door for her to change out of her uniform and hand it over to them. It was intended to be intimidating, but she and Dex had to hold back laughter throughout the experience. As if anyone would want to keep that dreadful uniform.

After the goons had left, they walked over to Le Rétro to meet Biagini and a few other people from the neighbourhood for a party to celebrate Annabelle's new life. They had been at the bar for a few hours, so Dex was watching Annabelle closely to make sure they didn't overstay her comfort level.

"So, you are alive after all." A body slid into the seat next to Dex and slipped an arm around his shoulder. It was Zeke Torres, one of the other residents of La Liberté and the unofficial leader of the occasional jam sessions that were held in the building's courtyard.

"The rumours of my death have been greatly exaggerated," Dex quoted, but Torres didn't seem to catch the reference as he laughed with gusto.

"We've got to get you back out for some tunes."

Dex nodded. René had been right — he was nesting. Even though living with Annabelle meant carefully making sure he wasn't overcrowding her, he wanted to spend as much time with her as possible. It was almost as if he thought he could future-proof their relationship by sheer quantity of proximity. But it was time to start getting back to the rest of his life. Especially now.

"You have something planned?"

Torres shook his head. "But all it takes is a decision. Let's say, two nights from now? Around sundown?"

Dex found himself already looking forward to tuning his cheap mandolin. "It's a date."

"Perfect!" Torres leaned over for an awkward but sincere hug and then stood up, albeit in a slightly wobbly manner. "I'll put up a notice and let the usual suspects know. It's going to be great!" He barely stumbled at all as he made his way to the door and out into the night.

"Got a date with a theremin?" Annabelle asked.

"Well, no, it's Zeke's theremin. I don't think he's into sharing." Dex said. "But yeah, we organized a thing for a couple days from now."

Annabelle smiled, her hand twitching as if to reach out

toward Dex, then growing still and staying on her lap. The smile also stayed. She was doing okay, but Dex figured they wouldn't be out much longer. "That's great. It's been too long."

"I know." His thought was cut off by a familiar figure walking toward the table. It was Jamie Eristo.

"Captain, it's nice to see you," they said, greeting René, then noticing Dex. "Oh, hi, how's it going?"

"Good," Dex said. "I saw the report on the mess from the other day. I'm glad they didn't fire the clerk."

Jamie nodded. "I sure wish we had a lead, though. It would be nice to give whoever did that a taste of their own medicine."

Dex could sense Annabelle looking at the newcomer, and turned to make the introductions. When he saw her face, though, he was surprised to see a glimmer of recognition.

"Uh, Annabelle, this is Jamie Eristo. They work with René, part of the street team."

She nodded but Dex could almost see the gears turning in her mind. Jamie turned toward her and a look of shock then confusion crossed their face. Then they smiled and said, "Annabelle. It's good to see you again. How do you know Dex and the captain?"

"Dex and I work together on the M City squad," Annabelle said and Dex felt his stomach drop out. Then she added, "And we're partners off the clock, too." She took a breath, and took Dex's hand, hanging on tightly. Dex knew she didn't want to touch him, to touch anyone or anything right now, but she did it anyway. Making a point. God, how he loved that woman.

Jamie grinned and said, "That's fantastic. Is he the one—" They stopped talking abruptly, seeming to realize that this line of questioning could go somewhere bad in a hurry, but Annabelle laughed and took the opportunity to retract her hand.

"Yeah, he's the one." She turned to look at him, and Dex forgot to breathe for a moment. "He is most definitely the one."

Jamie took the hint and made polite noises before beating a hasty retreat. Dex stood abruptly and announced, "I am taking the guest of honour home now. None of you are invited." There were some snickers and grins, and Biagini looked like he had a bon mot to impart, then decided against it. He just nodded silently and went back to his conversation.

"Thanks for helping me celebrate, everyone," Annabelle said as she stood. "I have no idea how this is all going to work, but at least I know I've got you all behind me."

"All right, this lot has had enough of you for one day," Dex said gruffly. "It's home time with you, young lady."

"Sir, yes, sir," Annabelle said in a tone of voice that did amazing things to Dex's insides. He waved at the table and they set off toward home.

THEY WALKED FOR SEVERAL blocks with nearly a metre gap between them, but by the time they were nearing the train station, Annabelle had moved closer. She curled her index finger around Dex's pinky and a sigh escaped from between his lips.

"That was fun," she said, "but I'm glad to be heading home."

"We could have held it in M City," Dex said. "Everyone would have understood."

"I know. But they're *out here* people and it was an *out here* thing we were celebrating. It was okay, really." She squeezed his finger. "I'm a lot more comfortable out here than I once was." She let Dex's finger slip out of her grasp, but stayed close by his side.

"So, Jamie..." Dex said.

"Yeah, that's a weird coincidence. Sure, Nice isn't enormous, but it's not like you run into the same people every day."

"Mmm..." Dex said.

"I mean, I haven't seen Jamie once since the clinic. I didn't even know they were part of René's team."

Dex started to put it all together. He didn't want to pry, not into parts of Annabelle's past that she didn't want to share, but also into Jamie's private life, which was none of his business. He was curious though.

"Were you two... close?"

Annabelle shook her head. "Not really. It was just the two of us getting work done, so we only had each other for company. Getting your body reshaped isn't just expensive — it can be quite unpleasant at times. I mean, there are plenty of stims to keep the pain at bay, but it's still surgery, right? And there's the mental part of it too."

"Sure," Dex said. When he'd first met Annabelle in the physical world, she was still wearing the male body she'd been born into. She had moved so much of her life into the virtual world that most of the time she forgot that her physical body didn't match the way she saw herself. But shortly after they began to become closer, she decided to "upgrade the meat" as she put it.

Dex had always worried that she did it for him, that if he hadn't been so resistant to living mainly online, she wouldn't have felt like she had to change a part of herself that she'd never really cared about. A part of herself that Dex would have loved regardless of its particular configuration.

"But you know, when you're cooped up in a tiny clinic room for a couple of days with one other person, you can't help but get to know them a little. Jamie was my best friend for those two days, but once we got out, that was it. It's funny, we never even swapped contact info. Didn't even occur to me and I guess they felt the same way." She stopped walking and turned to face Dex. "It was like maybe we didn't want to be reminded of our old bodies, our old lives? Of that point of transition in between what came before and what we have now? I don't know, maybe I'm overthinking it and it was just a friendship of convenience that we had no need to continue. Anyway," she grabbed Dex's hand and started walking again, "it was weird to see them again. Weird, but nice. I'm glad to see that things are going well for them."

"Yeah," Dex said, "they're a good detective."

Dex and Annabelle walked the rest of the way home in a companionable silence, but Dex couldn't help hearing Jamie's question in his mind.

"Is he the one?"

The one who *what*?

THE NEXT MORNING DEX was feeling the night before, but Annabelle wanted to get right into her new life as a freelancer. She'd already set up several meetings with potential clients and intended to be in M City for the whole day. She said she was perfectly happy to park at the table in the apartment, but after the previous night Dex thought giving her a little space was the right thing to do.

"I want to go check on a few things," he said, "I'll be back in a few hours."

"Okay," she answered, her focus already shifted to an invisible point in the distance. She was a better multitasker than Dex was, but even she wasn't going to be much of a conversationalist while she was busy online, so Dex slipped out of the apartment.

He walked over to the shop he'd investigated with Jamie, and he was impressed. There was no indication that anything had ever happened, although he didn't recognize the cashier working behind the counter. A bad feeling settled into his stomach and he asked, "Is Liisa working today?"

The clerk shook his head. "She's on nights now."

Dex smiled in relief but couldn't help but wonder if moving her to the night shift was a punishment. He almost wished he'd never suggested that the attack might have been directed toward her. Did Techloid have audio monitoring equipment on the external part of the store? It wasn't outside the realm of possibility. There was surely video at least inside the store. Which of course meant that they had more of a clue who had trashed the place than Jamie or Dex, but the files indicated that they hadn't even sent a low level security officer around.

Dex couldn't figure it out. Did head office care about the break-in or not? Did they blame Liisa, and if they did, why not fire her? There was something going on here that bothered him; it reminded him of the confusing events that happened in M City a few years ago. That, based on the incident with the tea shop, would still be happening if the crypto package they'd helped to distribute wasn't keeping attackers at bay.

Could it really be the same thing, only in reverse? Was he actually right — that there weren't any coincidences and it was all part of a single, grand strategy? Was Liisa's shop vandalized, not by some individuals out to get her in trouble or kids looking for cheap stims and snacks, but by some kind of misguided activists trying to even the playing field?

Did they think that they were the heroes of this story?

TWELVE

DEX WALKED TO A NEARBY PARK and found a shady spot under a tree. He paged over to the local squad's board and ran a search for cases similar to the break-in at the Techloid shop. There were about a dozen matches from the past month — nothing of significant value stolen, but property and time lost. On a hunch, Dex had his system run a background check on the establishments that had been hit, looking for patterns among their staff, locations, inventories — anything that might mark a connection.

While he waited for the results, he paged over to his local files and reviewed his visit to the disk block for sale. He'd had several follow-up messages from the sales agency, which he'd been studiously ignoring. He really ought to set up a filter to automatically shunt them to his oubliette, but then he wondered if now that he was on their radar there was a way to use that to his advantage.

He opened the latest message and composed a quick reply.

> Thanks for taking the time to show me this disk block. Before I make a decision, I'd like to see if there is anything similar that might be available. I'm interested in a single block, privately

traded. Please provide me with a list of suitable properties at your earliest convenience.

He sent it off, hoping that it was tempting enough for the agency to do the hunting for him. Surely S. Wu wasn't the only one of Nightingale's beneficiaries trying to sell their block. And Dex felt like if he could get eyes on a few more of them, he might be able to start seeing something of a pattern. Or at least, it might shake loose a new idea. He was fresh out at the moment.

As he refocused on his surroundings, he noticed a woman selling drinks from a small cart set up next to the Econoline vending machine. Dex didn't share René Biagini's love for artisanal food, but something made him veer toward the cart.

"What have you got?"

She smiled a salesperson's grin at him and launched into a well-practiced patter.

"I make several home-mixed drinks from real ingredients — today I have a berry cordial, a mint spritzer, fermented ginger tonic, a—"

Dex cut her off. "You can stop right there. I'll take the ginger, please."

"Sure thing." She reached into an insulated bin and removed a small polyglass bottle. She named a price which was triple what Dex would have paid for a drink from the machine, but he just nodded and passed his hand over her chip reader. His implant registered with a quiet *bleep* and the transfer was done. He popped the top off the tonic and took a sip.

"This is good," he said. "I have a neighbour who brews ginger beer sometimes, but this is different. Very nice."

"Thank you," she beamed, a real full smile that reached

her eyes, rather than her sales face. "I'm quite proud of this recipe."

Dex took another sip. "So, how did you get into this? It can't be easy standing out here all day hoping for a sale?"

She shrugged. "It's not, but I didn't have a lot of choice. I worked for a firm that did high end real food service — that's where I learned to do this — but about six months ago they were bought out by Econoline." She jerked her head toward the vending machine. "We were told that we would be folded in as a sub-brand, and everything went on as normal for a few weeks. But then the product lines got cut, staff were let go, and about a month ago they finally shut the whole unit down. 'Insufficient market share' we were told, but I don't think they ever intended to keep it going. It was one of those acquire-to-destroy moves."

"That's terrible," Dex said.

She nodded. "I was lucky. All of us who were based in Nice managed a lot better than some of the staff in other areas. At least here we have a street life, there's actually people around I can sell my goods to. So many places, people just train into work, train home again and spend all their off time in M City or in sims. I don't know what the people in those places did for work."

"Surely they could get another job at a different firm?"

"Probably not. It's specialty work and there isn't much turnover. As it is, this isn't enough for me," she gestured at her cart, "and I had to get a half time entry level office job for the bennies. Customer service rep." She wrinkled her nose.

"Been there," Dex said. "Hopefully this will pick up enough to be full time for you."

"That's the dream," she said, "but I don't see a long line of customers waiting behind you."

Dex looked around at the mostly empty park and nodded. "Well, here's hoping."

He lifted his half empty bottle toward her in a toast and set off toward La Liberté. He hadn't heard a story like hers before, but he wondered how common it was. How common it was becoming.

He passed a woman walking toward him in a Gractor uniform, entry level by the looks of it. He didn't think anything of it until he head her yell, "Get a real job." He turned to see her striding off past the woman with the drinks cart, whose face was red even though she carried on as if nothing had happened.

Dex flashed her a smile, wondering how often that happened. It was hard enough trying to make a go of a new business on your own without dealing with abuse. What was wrong with some people?

DEX WAS ENTERING THE courtyard of La Liberté when his system pinged with a message from the virtual property sales agency. They had two similar disk blocks available to view at his earliest convenience. No time like the present, he thought.

He pinged Annabelle to let her know that he was on his way back to the apartment and quickly received a message-free ACK response. That was good — she was busy.

He spiralled up the lift to their floor and tried to be as unobtrusive as possible entering the apartment. Even though he'd warned Annabelle, he knew that it was easy to be startled by unexpected noises in the physical world when you were focussed on something online.

He tiptoed around Annabelle, who was glassy-eyed at the

table, and grabbed a food brick and bottle of water before settling into the closet-office. He set up appointments with the sales office, which was happy to show him the other two properties immediately. One of the many advantages of using bots — they were always available at short notice.

Dex linked into the first site in the Kanzai district. He recognized it as one he'd passed several times on his way to or from the M City squad offices. It was hardly distinguishable from the block he'd seen in Quayside. The shops were the same only different — where the Quayside block had avatar customization shops, here there were a pair of cafés; the large space here was an art gallery, the office building was shinier and the sex bots were bespoke models for rent rather than sale. But all in all it was almost like the two disk blocks had been carved from a mould. Was that even a thing? He'd have to ask Annabelle later.

He looked around and made the right noises to the sales bot's sales pitch, then linked over to the other site. Again, the look and feel of the external rez matched the neighbourhood but the underlying configuration of the block was the same as the other two. He went through the motions with the sales bot then made his excuses and linked over to his own office.

Dex had taken snapshots of the façades and interior spaces he'd viewed and looked them over briefly to see if he could spot a pattern. Other than the obvious similarity between all three blocks, there was nothing that jumped out at him. He linked down to street level and walked quickly up the road, paying attention to the configuration of the various blocks. They were all somewhat different — Chandlers had the feel of an urban space that had evolved on its own, rather than being planned and managed — but Dex noticed several blocks that fundamentally matched the same configuration pattern. Was it just that there was a default M City block, a pre-configured disk image that was the simplest format to install? Or was there another connection, one that Dex couldn't see?

He linked back to his office and compiled his notes and files on the disk blocks for sale, then set up a search on his system to look for links. He could do it himself, of course, but he'd learned that machines were good for some things — better than people, even himself. He didn't mind outsourcing some of the drudge work, especially when it was a long shot like this.

There wasn't anything else he could think to do on this case, so he checked on the results from his search on the local cases of burglary and vandalism. Dex's system search had turned up a virtual file folder stuffed with data. This was the downside to automation — a machine doesn't quite know what is a useful correlation and what isn't. But it was a place to start.

There were no obvious signs of a pattern — the locations that had been hit were scattered all throughout the region. Dex guessed that the only reason the list ended at the local boundary was because, beyond that, the squad simply didn't know about them. They were all minor events — low value but high annoyance. The Techloid shop Dex had visited was typical. In fact, it was notable that at none of the events in his list had anything of significant value been taken. More damage was done than items were stolen in all the incidents.

It bothered him. Sure, there were plenty of people who enjoyed a bit of pointless violence, who just wanted to feel the rush of seeing shit break. But there had to be more people who were desperate for a meal or a fresh one-piece, who'd be more motivated to take something valuable than simply trash the joint. They'd all been working on the assumption that this was the work of street low-lifes; the break-ins all had those ear-marks. But then why not line their pockets while they were at it?

Dex flipped through the analysis to see if there were any interesting patterns, but it all felt random. Then something in Appendix C caught his eye. It was a listing of the security departments that had gotten involved at some point in the process. Mostly, they had been notified as part of the business's standard procedure, but only one had actually sent anyone out to investigate. That had been a two-person team from Empyre, the umbrella corporation which owned the QuikStop brand of shops.

Dex flipped over to their report, such as it was. They'd spent ten minutes sifting through the mess at a smash and grab that was ten times more smash than grab. He checked the details on the incident — it was a QuikStop outlet in a commercial zone near the airport. And it was one of the first to be reported. He went back to the appendix and looked at the list of security departments notified. There were the names of several firms, but Dex recognized a few as subsidiaries of Empyre. He plugged all the names into his system and drummed his fingertips on the scarred wood of his desk as he waited.

He shook his head in disbelief. Almost all the security teams named were arms of either Empyre or Techloid. A quick search on the names of each of the businesses targeted confirmed it. Aside from three outliers, which didn't entirely match the rest of the cases in other ways, every business that had been hit was ultimately under the umbrella of either Techloid or Empyre.

Apparently, someone really was on a mission to disrupt

the two biggest corporations supplying consumables to the entire world.

"Well," Dex thought, leaning back in his chair and planting his big black wingtips on the desk, "at least I can't fault them for setting their sights too low."

THIRTEEN

ZEKE TORRES ALWAYS REMINDED DEX a bit of someone deep in the throes of a focus™-based stim cocktail. He was pretty sure it was actually Torres's natural state, rather than chemically induced, but the man didn't do anything in half measures. Until he'd shifted apartments to move in with Annabelle, Dex had lived next door to Zeke, but they'd kept different hours so tended to see each other only at the irregular jam sessions in the courtyard. When he'd changed his hours to match the rest of Europa, it hadn't seemed to make an impact on his social schedule.

It had been some time since Dex had met up with Zeke, Noemi Petersen and the other musicians who lived in the complex for an hour or two of a pick-up concert, and he was rusty. He found himself a beat behind when they switched to a new song, he stuck to keeping a straight melody line rather than noodling around with harmonies, and his fretting fingers ached. He didn't mind — he'd missed this.

Dex's lack of practice didn't appear to faze Torres, whose eyes remained serenely closed while his hands danced over his theremin in complex patterns. A tiny woman Dex didn't recognize had joined them with a small box with which she created both electronic beats and the sounds of analogue percussion, and Noemi sat between them filling in the gaps with her flute. It was an odd instrumental mix, but they must have sounded all right, since the small group of listeners had grown substantially since they began.

Dex knew that Annabelle had been there when they began to play, but he wouldn't have begrudged her leaving when the space on the courtyard turf became crowded. He didn't have the confidence to look out to see while he was playing, and it wouldn't have mattered either way. If she wasn't here in person she'd be listening on a feed. If it hadn't been for her gift of the cheap mandolin several years ago, he wouldn't be here playing at all. He knew that she knew how much this meant to him.

By the time Zeke Torres opened his eyes, sighed, and switched off his theremin, Dex didn't think he could straighten out the fingers of his left hand.

"Damn, I'm out of practice," he said to Noemi who smiled.

"It's quick to go," she said, "but quick to come back, too."

Dex should have been embarrassed that she'd noticed his playing errors, but somehow it didn't seem to matter. In the hour they'd been playing it was as if time had, not stopped exactly, but stretched into an elastic wave on which Dex had been lightly buoyed. It was simultaneously refreshing and exhausting.

Dex packed away the mandolin in its case and was startled to hear a familiar voice say, "Have fun?"

He looked up into Annabelle's face, the dark eyes she'd gone back to wearing recently appearing to nearly shine down on him. A smile spread across his face.

"You stayed to the bitter end?"

She nodded. "You aren't the only one who missed this, you know."

He was taken aback. "No, I didn't know. I guess I thought you only came along to these things for, you know, moral support or something."

Annabelle laughed and rolled her eyes. "I don't like being a music groupie, Dex, I like hearing you play. I like seeing you play. And, sure, I like seeing you be happy, too. But it's all those things."

He stood and slipped an arm around her, carefully checking for any stiffness or other indication that he should back off, but none came. "You have strange taste," he said. "I like that."

"That makes two of us."

ANNABELLE WENT BACK TO the apartment to let Dex socialize, but he found that the exhaustion had begun to overtake the exhilaration and begged off after half an hour. He pinged Annabelle to let her know he was on his way up, and noticed that there was a case request for him from Mack Larsen. He'd have to look at that later — he wasn't up for anything more than a good nights' sleep.

"You're picking up my bad habits," Annabelle said when Dex flopped onto the bed. "You're the one who is supposed to love hanging out with the meat sacks." It could have sounded spiteful, but there were equal measures of affection and concern in her tone.

"Oh, I still love my meat sacks," Dex said, laughing. "But I am beat. My hands feel like they've been pounded with mallets and my brain is like one of those green gobs that washes up on the beach sometimes."

"Ew."

"Exactly." He leaned over to kiss Annabelle and it went on longer than he expected. Eventually she broke away and Dex said, "The flesh is weak, I'm afraid."

"I know," she answered, "that's why I prefer pixels."

"Well, right now my pixels are weak, too," Dex said. "I'm about ready to pass out here."

Annabelle slipped out of bed and dimmed the lights. As she closed the door, she said, "'Night, honey," but Dex was already asleep.

AFTER A DEEP AND DREAMLESS sleep, Dex woke early the next morning. He let Annabelle sleep and padded into the closet office to get a jump on the day. He was curious about Larsen's message.

It was a desperate-sounding request from the proprietor of a holiday sim agency, one Izzy Marcula. Apparently, several days previously her M City landlord had contacted her about a supposed breach of service. The landlord, Blockchain, was one of the smaller data block companies, and they claimed that some code within one of Marcula's sims was exceeding the tolerances of her contract and had unceremoniously cut off access to her instantiation.

In her report to Larsen, she said that the offending sim was one which no one had ordered in months, but she had her technician check the code just in case, and found nothing untoward. That was only one part of the problem, though. The real concern was that she had contacted Blockchain dozens of times to try and resolve the issue and get access to her storefront and rez space, but she had been met with silence. She had admin access to her data but potential customers were met with a blank wall and a 404 when they tried to access her agency.

Obviously, there wouldn't be anything for Dex to see if he went to her M City location, so he invited her to meet him in his office. On the face of it, this was just another customer service nightmare, but given the continued attacks on M City establishments, Dex wondered if perhaps something malicious had gotten into her sim code. This kind of situation had been common in the past, and while the crypto package that the organization had distributed had ended the proliferation of these kind of attacks, perhaps the culprits had found a new way around their defences.

That thought disturbed Dex, but he couldn't discount its likelihood. He knew that incursion and detection were in a mutually escalating and evolving battle of technology. With every new attack, a new defence had to be developed, which then spawned attackers attempting to circumvent those new roadblocks. The best they could hope for was that the attackers would get bored with the attempt. Dex had hoped that this was what had happened, but now he was unconvinced. Which was terrible news.

The simulated glass in Dex's office door rattled as someone on the other side knocked.

"Come in."

The door opened and an expensive-looking avatar glided into Dex's office. The body was tall and thin, a spray of dark hair adding even more height, the face's complexion a bright blue. Unlike many unnaturally coloured avatar skins, this wasn't a uniform overlay of colour, but rather matched the subtle differences in hue that humans normally had on their bodies. Only it was blue. A very well-done piece, if a bit flashy for Dex's taste.

"I'm Izzy Marcula." She held out a blue hand with eerily long fingers for Dex to shake. He did, then gestured to the wooden chair opposite his desk. Marcula sat and Dex grabbed the file he'd downloaded from the squad's board.

"I've got the information you provided to my colleagues here," Dex said, "but can you go over it again for me? When did you discover that your access had been cut off?"

"It's been six days now," Marcula said, her voice tight. Dex could empathize — being locked out of both your place of business and your means of production was enough to drive anyone to a rage. "I've begun negotiations with a new host. I just can't wait around for Blockchain to get back to me — if they're ever going to."

"When was the last time you heard from one of their representatives?"

She took a deep breath. "Arguably, never?" Dex frowned and she explained. "The initial notification read like an automated message. You know, 'Our monitoring software detected a fault in one of your applications and your account has been suspended pending an investigation.' If an actual human being had any involvement, I'd be surprised."

"And then?"

"And then silence. I've responded multiple times, including sending the results of my own analysis, trying get an answer. Even just to get someone to give me the details of this supposed fault. I mean, if there is something wrong, I'm happy to fix it, but I'm becoming more and more convinced that there is no fault. That they're just using it as an excuse to dump me from my contract."

Dex scanned the papers on his desk. "I see here that you

have nearly 18 months left on your contract. It was pre-paid, is that correct?"

"Yes." Marcula's avatar remained placid but the voice that came from it was anything but calm. "But at this point I don't see how I'm going to get anything out of them. Not a reinstatement of my account, not my money back. I've yet to receive anything but automated acknowledgements of my support requests with vague reassurances that my ticket is in the queue."

Dex frowned. "You have backups?"

Marcula nodded. "And I do have admin access to my files on the data block. It's just public access which has been locked."

"I see." Dex closed the file folder and took a breath. "Well, I have to be honest here. I'm not at all certain that there is anything I'll be able to do for you in this situation. Most rez space hosting agreements have a clause indemnifying the leaseholder from faults arising from the lessee's scripts, and if they don't actually want to keep your account I don't see how we can compel them to respond."

"That's what I thought," Marcula said, "but I figured I ought to try."

Dex nodded. "I still want to look into this. We might not get a favourable outcome for you, but this is very strange behaviour. There might be something else going on, something that we can stop from happening to someone else. And, who knows, if this turns out to be a third-party attack against Blockchain, we might be able to get some redress. I just wouldn't count on it."

"Thank you." Marcula stood, her hair brushing the office's ceiling. "I'm going to focus on finding a replacement host. I can't afford to be closed for business much longer."

"I understand." Dex shook her hand and said, "I'll let you know if we find anything." She nodded and left the office.

Dex slumped down into his chair. He hated giving people bad news, but he didn't see any likely resolution to this case that ended up with Marcula getting her space or her payment back. If they were playing dirty pool, Blockchain had been clever about it. Accusing Marcula's code of having a critical fault absolved them from locking her out. Refusing to respond to her could be explained away as being overloaded with enquiries. If they stalled long enough, most anyone in this situation would eventually just get another rez space. There was only so much time and energy a person could put into fighting for an eighteen month refund.

But if this was the scheme, what was the end game? Dumping Marcula as a customer? Why? Surely they had to know that she would go public with her story, which would give future potential customers pause. That gave Dex an idea and he ran a quick search for public posts about Blockchain. Maybe this wasn't an isolated incident.

FOURTEEN

IT WAS MID-AFTERNOON, DEFINITELY still the workday, but Dex and René Biagini had decided that there was no point in being essentially your own boss if you couldn't give the staff a break every once and again. René had a small bowl of some revolting looking organic food substance in front of him and Dex had a glass of Jamaica's Best and ginger. It was a far cry from a real dark n' stormy but he didn't feel like he deserved the good stuff when he was just skiving off for a few hours. He hadn't even solved anything.

"So they are literally all Empyre or Techloid shops?" Biagini asked, practically caressing his meal with a fork.

"All but three and if you really drill into those ones, they don't match the pattern. One had a lot of stock stolen, one was barely even disrupted by a small graffiti tag and the third was an independent player who'd had some shady business associates before she tried to go straight." Dex shook his head. "The ones that all fit the pattern are all either owned by

Techloid or by Empyre."

René took a bite of his lumpy, green stew and closed his eyes. It was a look of pleasure which Dex recognized, but didn't understand. That stuff looked like it oozed out from under a rock on the beach. When René was done his foodgasm, he scowled. "So you think it's a vigilante? Sticking it to the man, something like that?"

"Maybe?" Dex swirled his drink in the glass, watching carbonation bubbles float to the surface. "Could be a revenge thing. Someone angry at losing a job?"

"I don't know," René said, a skeptical look on his face. "If it were only one firm being targeted, I could see that, but two? And both of them seemed to start being hit at about the same time. It's a lot for one disgruntled ex-employee to do."

"Yeah, I don't see this being a one-person operation," Dex said. "The geographical area alone makes that improbable. And I'm convinced this isn't a local phenomenon either. Any word from your compadres on other squads?"

René shook his head. "I only put out the request yesterday and I couldn't in good conscience mark it urgent. It could be a while."

"Well, I'm operating under the assumption that this is happening all over, and it's being done by a group. A pretty well organized group, to boot." He began ticking off points on his fingers. "One: none of the attacks have been caught on internal surveillance video in clear enough rez to get an identity. Two: Even though several of the targeted businesses keep long hours, none were hit when there were any staff on duty. Three: if you're hiring local thugs to run a smash and don't grab, odds are that someone will get stickier fingers than they are supposed to and take something valuable. That hasn't happened. Four: I... don't really have a point number four. I just feel in my guts that this is part of a well-coordinated, centrally-managed operation. It feels almost corporate."

Dex shrugged and took a slug of his drink.

"I will admit that your guts have been right more often than not," René conceded. "Maybe when we hear from the other teams it will give us something more to go on. But I agree, something smells fishy."

Dex wrinkled his nose. "René, it's your lunch."

René laughed. "You are such a philistine, Andersson Dexter. It's a good thing you're so pretty, or I don't know why I'd keep company with you."

"Jesus, René." Dex felt his cheeks heating up and he cursed the fact that René still managed to embarrass him. He also cursed the fact that he couldn't manage to keep the smile off his face. "Save it for an appreciative audience, will you?"

René shrugged and said, "Oh, I know you appreciate it. Everyone likes to be admired, even you Mister Hard Ass." He waggled his eyebrows and Dex failed to keep the laugh that had been brewing inside. The two broke into a fit of giggles loud enough to make the people at the next table look over. Which didn't help matters at all.

IT WAS STILL EARLY WHEN Dex left Le Rétro; he knew he ought to get a bit more work in before heading home. He decided to walk down to the beach. Maybe having the ocean on the other side of his visual overlay would be the kind of soothing influence that would jog some ideas. As he neared the waterfront, the scent of the sea assaulted his nostrils. It was both pleasant and not, intensely organic. Something smelled fishy, indeed.

He was smirking at his own joke when he noticed something odd. The beach wasn't terribly wide but it was long, stretching from the airport all the way to the seaport at the other end of the bay. While the beach area near the town site had the usual selection of street vendors and sun worshippers, Dex could see that in both directions there were pockets of what looked like dug outs or makeshift tents. Dex started walking toward the seaport, curiosity having gotten the better of him.

As he got closer, he realized that he'd been right — they were impromptu shelters. He approached one and saw that it was a large sheet of variplastic draped over some boxes and bins. There was movement inside, but Dex didn't want to startle the occupant, so he kept on walking. Several metres away was another makeshift beach hut, this one more robustly constructed with printed panels to make rudimentary walls and a roof.

Dex turned to walk back toward town. They were essentially streeters — people who had no corporate or private accommodation, scrounging for whatever they could. Every city had them, some to a greater or lesser extent than others. He'd seen more here in Nice than he had back in Namerica, which he assumed was due to the favourable climate. It was a lot easier to live outdoors in a place that never got close to freezing.

But this beach community was even more extensive than he'd realized. He mentally revised the number of streeters in Nice up by a large margin. It was... disturbing. He thought about the break-in at the Techloid shop and Liisa's fear of being fired over it. He wondered if that had been the result in some of the other cases. Is that why there were so many more people out here?

ANNABELLE WAS STILL WORKING when Dex got back to the apartment, which gave him twinge of guilt over his afternoon break with Biagini. He slipped into the closet office and linked into M City. He found his avatar behind his desk, a new file folder in his inbox. It had a slight luminous quality which meant that he hadn't yet opened it.

He grabbed it and scanned the contents. It was the analysis of the disk blocks for sale that he'd toured with the agency sales bot. He skimmed over the technical details which meant little to him, but his eyes caught on the list of tenants. He'd written the search parameters to drill down into whatever detail was available and like a good robot his system had complied. The full ownership details for every tenant were listed, including private investors, parent companies, and shell corporations. It was mostly uninteresting, except for one common feature: each of the disk blocks housed a tenant which was ultimately a subsidiary of the Oyuba Corporation.

Dex did a search of the tenants of the block Zahara Zhang now owned to see if any of them could be traced back to Oyuba. Bingo. One of the seemingly independent cafés was actually an Oyuba subsidiary.

So, how was Oyuba involved? Dex did some quick digging and was surprised to find that they had several rez space hosting arms. So, why would their subsidiaries lease from private blocks? It didn't make any sense.

A quiet knock on the closet door derailed Dex's train of thought.

"I'll be out in a minute," he called and logged out of M

City. Annabelle was digging through the chiller drawer and came up with a pair of hot meal packets. Dex nodded, not knowing what they contained. He'd never really cared about food and left it to Annabelle get what she liked. When he'd lived on his own it was nothing but economy sized cases of food bricks and that was good enough for him.

Annabelle set their dinner in the zapper, then said, "Sorry I worked so late. I'm not doing a good job of setting time boundaries for myself."

Dex grinned and slipped into his chair at the small pull-down table. "I know what you mean," he said. "I always thought there were lot of great things about working for myself, but I can't deny that the boss is an asshole."

Annabelle laughed. "You calling me an asshole?"

"Of course not," Dex said, holding up his hands in a gesture of supplication. "You were the one complaining about management."

She chuckled as the zapper dinged. She pulled out the meal packages and set them on the table. They were the fancy kind, that had three different flavour units. The package was designed to heat them all individually, so the liquid-stew part was piping hot, while the mushy green stuff was just this side of warm. At least it wasn't as off-putting as René's bowl of... whatever it was.

"So, how is it going?" Dex asked after a mouthful of green mush. It looked gross but it tasted okay.

"Good, I think." She pushed her food around with her spoon and looked thoughtful. "Stella Bish hooked me up with two gigs, neither of them a full load. But between them..." She made a face. "It's more than I can do in a normal day."

"Can't you just put one of them off? Work them sequentially?"

She shook her head. "Of course, they're both time-sensitive. One is patching the security for a training lab. Every minute that it's not done they're vulnerable. And the other one is just cosmetic, but it's for a rez installation that's been booked to open for months. And it's meant to go live in less than a week."

"Jeez," Dex said, "that wasn't really fair of Bish to lay those both on you." Annabelle looked up at Dex through her hair. He knew that expression. "You volunteered."

"They were my first job offers," she protested. "I didn't want to say no. And besides, I figured that if I put in a little extra effort in up front, that it would look good for me down the road. Happy clients and all that."

"Uh huh." Dex shook his head and tried to conceal his grin. It was typical Annabelle. And probably a smart move.

"What about you?" she asked. "Any news on Captain Zhang's mysterious benefactor?"

Dex explained what he'd turned up about Oyuba. "I can't be sure that the second blocks I viewed are even part of this inheritance," he said, "but it all feels connected, you know?"

Annabelle nodded, gesturing for him to go on.

"Oyuba is huge online — they probably control close to half the rez space in M City, plus all their other holdings. Sure, those umbrella corporations like to keep their different divisions separate, but I can't see any reason why one arm of Oyuba is paying rent to another arm of what is essentially the same organization. But it also seems totally improbable that the café and brothel divisions of Oyuba are paying some other company for rez space. Yet, that's how it appears. These disk blocks are really for sale and from everything I can find they are being sold by private individuals. It just doesn't make any sense."

"Hmm." Annabelle pursed her lips. "These big companies usually leave the day to day operations to the subs. I wonder if all of the blocks you've been looking at were part of one subsidiary but then something happened to it? Maybe it was sold off, or dissolved or something? A bunch of disk blocks are worth a ton of money, but let's be honest, they're small beans to an outfit like Oyuba."

"Yeah, you might be on to something," Dex said. "I should be able to take a look at the historical records, not for the blocks themselves, but for each tenant. That might shed a little light on things."

Annabelle grinned and took Dex's hand. "Glad I could help." She squeezed and let go, but then left her hand on his. "You know, I've missed this."

"Dinner?"

"No. Talking shop, noodling about cases. I mean, technically what you and I do is pretty different, but really it's all the same. Solving puzzles."

"You do always help me look at things from a different perspective."

She grinned. "A different perspective sounds good. How does horizontal grab you?"

FIFTEEN

DEX HAD A HARD TIME FOCUSING on work the next morning, but he gave it a good try. Annabelle had been teaching him how to keep part of his attention on the physical world while active in M City. He wasn't good at it and it felt extremely odd, but there were a few activities where it was particularly useful. Given Annabelle's preference for the virtual and Dex's opposite proclivity, it was a skill worth working on. They'd had an extensive practice session last night before falling asleep.

Now he was back in M City, trying to focus on the interior of his closet office back in Nice while still being able to read the files on his desk. He could do it if he really put his mind to it, but then he found that couldn't remember what he'd just read. Maybe this was a skill that should be contained to the bedroom. And the living room and kitchen and...

He grinned to himself. He was feeling pretty good when his messenger pinged. It was a file, not a call, since his desk phone didn't ring. He looked over at his in tray and saw a file materialize. He grabbed it and flipped it open.

It was the final report on the explosion at de Gaulle. Dex scanned it, his eyes getting caught on a word he hadn't expected to see. Fatality. There was one fatality recorded as a direct result of the incident. That can't be right, he thought, then read on. It was true that the injuries reported had only been minor, but the person who had sustained burns was not employed. He was a streeter who had been sleeping in the park and since he had no employment he also had no access to a med clinic. Left untreated, his injuries had apparently become infected. He'd been found dead in an alley only two blocks away from de Gaulle.

His name was Lennox Sessa. Dex committed the name to memory, then focussed his anger to try to get through the rest of the report.

The incident was being ruled an accident, but there were several caveats. The chain of events leading to the explosion was determined to be a case of bad luck — the heat from the overcharged power bank had been just enough to ignite the construction materials, which ordinarily wouldn't have been left there, but a windstorm had forced the construction crew to use the shelter of the power bank.

The overcharging of the power bank in the first place, on the other hand, was suspicious. There were multiple levels of safeguards in place to prevent that behaviour from occurring — not only was a flammable power bank unsafe, it was also entirely not cost effective. But the safeguards had all been remotely disabled. Every last one of them. It was as if someone were just waiting for the bank to overheat and burst.

The company who owned the power bank, Electrois, had apparently rebooted their entire safety system after the event, ensuring that their other power banks were protected properly. They refused to provide any additional information, but the supposition was that their entire fleet of power banks had been affected. It was sheer luck that only one had failed.

Dex pushed the file away, a sour feeling beginning to grow in his belly. This wasn't anything like the rash of vandalism — the MOs were entirely different. One was the work of brazen, street level hoodlums, the other was behind-the-scenes cracker work. But it felt like they were connected. The results were the same — disrupting the day-to-day operations of arms of the big firms.

On a hunch, Dex looked up Electrois, Techloid and Empyre to see if any of them were actually subsidiaries of a larger organization. Empyre came back negative — they were the parent. But the nasty feeling in his guts intensified when Dex saw that Electrois and Techloid were actually both owned by Vertisales.

Someone was targeting Empyre and Vertisales, and it was a coordinated, meticulous effort. The word that came to mind was "professional." How had he missed an organization like this? Dex was extremely well-connected within the small but growing resistance to the firms' control. At least, he'd always thought that he was. But what if he and the people he worked with weren't the only ones trying to change the balance of power. What if they weren't even the most effective?

Surely there had to be some crossover between the two groups. Dex's organization was mostly concerned about keeping M City accessible and these new vigilantes seemed to be confining their efforts on the physical world, but even people like Annabelle had a foot in each camp. Most people had contacts and business in both places.

He prepared a report with his hypothesis and sent it on a wide band to the squads he had access to, asking them to forward it on. Separately, he sent messages to Zahara Zhang, Mack Larsen and René Biagini to ask for a meeting. He wasn't sure the three of them had ever met before, but they were the squad captains whose ears he had and Dex was convinced that the more people who were looking into this, the better off they would be.

He had no moral problem with vigilantism. Arguably, he and the rest of the people who worked in his organization were guilty of just that. The closest thing to a rule of law were the policies and regulations set out by each company to govern its employees and the few areas where the firms agreed between themselves to act a certain way. And there was no doubt that Dex and his peers acted outside of what little law existed.

Dex was also no stranger to using violence or its threat to deter bad behaviour, and he didn't lose any sleep over that, either. He'd never cracked anyone's head who hadn't done worse themselves. Sure, it wasn't the best solution, but it was a solution and sometimes that was all you could do. He had no illusions about his own dubious ethics, but this seemed all wrong to him.

He recalled the anachronistic old saw that you had to break a few eggs to make an omelette — that collateral damage was a natural price one might have to pay in a fight. He got it; everything in life was a trade off. But it seemed to him that the attacks on the shops and businesses were disproportionately affecting ordinary people who were just caught up in the crossfire.

People being forced to work unpaid overtime or potentially even being fired was out of proportion, too. Dex thought of all those people living on the beach, the people on the street he'd seen sleeping under broken down cartons or selling their few possessions for whatever euros they could get. How many of them were made jobless and homeless because their employer blamed them for letting an attack happen on their shift?

If it was even one, that was one too many.

And as for the sabotage of the power banks, it was only random chance that no one had been killed at the point of the de Gaulle explosion. That anyone had been hurt at all seemed to Dex to be an unacceptable side effect, and then that someone had ultimately died — that was unconscionable.

It was not Lennox Sessa's fault that he was in the wrong place at the wrong time. But what happened to him was someone's fault. And Dex meant to find that person.

DEX HAD INVITED ANNABELLE to his meeting with the squad captains, but she begged off. "Too busy with work," she messaged. "Plus, I don't know anything about this. I doubt I'd be any help."

Even if she wasn't up to speed, tracking down these vigilantes seemed like a more valuable use of her time than a glorified paint job or even fixing some training lab's security patch. But he had pushed her into going freelance and he knew that when she did something, she did it right. And just because he was feeling slightly paranoid, that didn't mean that she had to drop everything to hold his hand.

"I'll fill you in later," he messaged back and linked over to the M City squad offices. Larsen had booked one of the fancy meeting rooms, and he was already there with Susana Bells, his number two. As soon as Dex saw them he had a flash of panic. What if he was totally overreacting? He had no solid proof for his theory; in fact, it was built on one piece of circumstantial evidence on top of another. Was he just wasting everybody's time?

Zahara Zhang walked through the door and extended a hand to Larsen. "Good to see you again, Mack. How are things going around here?"

"Can't complain," he said. "We're keeping the wolves at bay, at least."

Dex was spared from listening to any more of Larsen's clichés by René's arrival. At first, Dex didn't recognize him. They had never met in M City, so Dex wasn't prepared for Biagini's avatar — it was nearly a clone of a popular androgynous escort bot. Of course, being the sexiest avatar in the room was classic Biagini, so Dex wasn't entirely surprised when he saw his friend's name hover over the avatar. Knowing who was who, Dex turned off the overlay and gestured for everyone to sit at the long boardroom table.

"I suppose you're all wondering why I called you here today," he said, to Biagini's smirk and Zhang's long-suffering sigh. "Have you all had a chance to look at that file I sent around?"

There were nods all around the table and Biagini said, "I've got something to add to that file. Just this morning I got confirmation that attacks on Techloid and Empyre businesses fitting the pattern of what we've seen in Nice are, indeed, happening in jurisdictions all over Europa and Namerica." Dex felt a download drop into his system.

Zahara Zhang nodded. "We've had several cases in the last month. Nothing much stolen, but a lot of mess and disruption. It took a while to correlate, because many of the affected shops didn't contact anyone — they just cleaned up the mess and moved on."

Mack Larsen frowned. "I understand that you want to be thorough, but I have to point out that we haven't seen anything like this in here. Of course, neither Techloid nor Empyre have strong holdings in M City. So that would add another point in favour of the idea that this is specifically targeted at those two firms."

"It's not Techloid," Dex broke in, "not entirely, anyway." He explained the connection with Vertisales and the incident at de Gaulle. "I am convinced that whoever is behind this had no idea that there would be an explosion. It was, as much as I hate to admit it, just an unfortunate coincidence. But one person has already died. Something has to be done before someone else gets hurt." There were several nods around the room. "It seems to me that there is pretty clearly an orchestrated effort to disrupt these two companies. What we need to do is find out who's behind it."

Susana Bells was the first to say what Dex guessed they all had been thinking. "Do you think it might be some of the same people we worked with before? When we distributed the initial package to decentralize M City?"

It was a rhetorical question, but Biagini answered it anyway. "Seems likely. By necessity, we were working with people who have no loyalty to the firms, some of whom actively want to reduce their influence. I mean, let's be candid — all of us sitting here in this room could be described that way. I can imagine that some of the people we dealt with might be inclined to take more direct action, sure." He ran his hands over his smooth, pretty avatar's face. "Honestly, if I hadn't seen the spillover effects myself, I might be inclined to approve of it, too. Sitting around complaining that you don't like the way the world is being run never solved anything."

"This isn't the way to do it," Dex said.

"I know, I know," Biagini answered. "I'm only saying I can see the appeal. And it's easy to start with a noble cause then get a bit carried away with the execution. Especially if you have a lot of people involved."

"And there must be an awful lot of people involved," Zhang said. "Look at how many places have been affected." She shook her head. "I don't know how this has been kept quiet, given how many people this would take. Even if it's say, a team of two in each location, that's still at least hundred individuals."

"Unless they are traveling," Dex said to looks of confusion. "Let's say that this project is your full time gig. No, I don't know how that would work financially, but putting that aside for a moment, if my daily grind is pulling jobs like this, I bet I could travel to most of the locations in Europa over the course of when these attacks happened."

"Well," Larsen said, "it would easy enough to find out if that were possible. Give me a minute." His avatar froze for a moment, and when he reanimated, a large chart materialized on the table in front of him.

"I've plotted out all the events from Biagini's report, grouped by an easy day's travel. Dex is right, this could all be done with a few small teams working full out."

He spread the chart on the table and Dex was amazed to clearly see the pattern. A shop would be hit in one location, then the next day a similar event would take place in a nearby area. The pattern would continue in a loop, resulting in another attack in the first location several days later. It made each attack in an individual jurisdiction appear somewhat random, but when it was laid out like this the pattern was obvious.

"Well," Biagini said. "That was unexpected."

SIHTEEN

"I DON'T BELIEVE IT," ANNABELLE SAID, when they'd gone over to Monte's after the meeting.

"But here, look," Dex said, trying to keep the wounded feeling from coming out in his voice. He spread the chart out on the table, momentarily making their drinks disappear. "The pattern is really clear. I just — it can't possibly be a coincidence. Not in all these different places."

"Sorry, " Annabelle said, "I didn't mean that I don't believe *you;* I'm sure you're right. What I mean is..." She gestured vaguely, as if trying to draw her thoughts in the air. "What the fuck? Who is doing this?"

"Oh." Dex recalibrated his emotions. Of course, that was what she meant. "I don't know. That's the big question, right? Even if there's only a couple of people involved in each area, this still seems like the kind of operation that would be tough to hide. If I were out there, sticking it to the man like this, I'd have a hard time keeping that to myself. And I'm probably better at keeping a secret than the next person."

Annabelle nodded. "Not that you'd do something like this," she said. "Aside from the moral issues, the ROI seems terrible."

"Huh?"

"The return on investment. This is a lot of effort — the travel alone costs both money and time. This chart only works if the people involved are doing this as their full-time gig. And it's not like they are repaying their costs with stolen goods."

"So they have a benefactor, maybe? There are more than a few independent business owners out there. Maybe one of them took it into their head to finance a minor coup." He was thinking of Stella Bish, though he doubted this was in her wheelhouse.

Annabelle obviously had the same thought. "I don't think this is the work of anyone we know," she said. "And again, I have to ask, what's the ROI? What are these attacks really accomplishing? I checked and it's not like either Vertisales or Empyre seems to really be hurt by this. They both have so many subsidiaries and business lines that whoever is doing this would have to firebomb all the Quikstops in the world before it made a dent."

"I hope it doesn't come to that," Dex said. "Besides, it's not like there haven't been any real world consequences." He described what had happened with Liisa. "I'm convinced all those new streeters are no coincidence. The storefront attacks might not be hurting people directly, but they aren't benign either. That's why we have to find out who is doing this and get them to stop."

"There's no reason to believe that's where this is heading. De Gaulle was awful, but it was an accident and there hasn't been anything else that was dangerous to life or limb. It's all been property damage so far."

"Hang on," Dex said. "Something has been bothering me

since we found out about Vertisales. I know that name. I'm sure I've heard it somewhere before." He ran a search on the news sites, something he probably should have done long ago. It didn't take long to find it.

"Jesus Christ. I read this around the time of the de Gaulle explosion, but I didn't connect it. There was an industrial accident in Samerica. Four people were hurt when scaffolding failed at a Vertisales construction site."

"What are the odds that it was sabotage?" Annabelle asked.

"Not zero, that's for fucking sure. These people have to be stopped, Annabelle. Before Lennox Sessa becomes just one name among many."

Annabelle nodded gravely and had the rendering system clean up their table. A fresh drink materialized before her and she picked up the glass. "So, how are we going to find them?"

Dex sighed and lit a cigarette. He blew a plume of blue smoke toward the ceiling. "That's what I was hoping you'd be able to tell me."

THE NEXT MORNING DEX didn't even bother linking in to M City. He parked himself in the closet office and banged out a virtual pile of communications. He'd been part of the physical distribution network when they had disseminated the code to help keep M City open, and had met dozens of people throughout Europa who were concerned about the firms consolidating power. It had felt like something out of a historical spy vid — all codenames and cloak-and-dagger passphrases.

Once the secure system had been set up, though, the need

for secret handshakes was over. A few of the people Dex had met had messaged him to thank him for his work, so he had contact information for them. He scrounged through his system looking for those details now.

He found it difficult to word a message essentially asking if they knew of anyone who might be part of a secret organization bent on wreaking destruction. He tried a version that made it sounds like he wanted to join up, but it felt wrong. He settled on a "just the facts"-style query.

He knew there was a good chance he was tipping his hand; if any of his contacts were part of the group, they would know that someone was on to them and switch up their tactics. To a certain extent, Dex was fine with that if it meant that they quit their attacks. He had no strong desire to see them face the consequences of their actions, he simply wanted the collateral damage to stop.

With that done, he logged into the M City squad board. Larsen had offered to host the files for this case — ironically, since his was the only jurisdiction unaffected. But that meant that none of the other squads held precedence. Generally, there wasn't much squabbling or jurisdictional wrangling, but it wasn't unheard of. This solution put a stop to that before it could begin. As much as Dex still couldn't find it in his heart to like Mack Larsen, he had to admit that the man was good at his job.

He paged around the case file and perused the rest of the team's efforts so far. They'd covered a lot of ground in a short time. That was one of the advantages of having a lot of people involved. Dex wasn't the only one with underworld contacts, and a metric flurry of messages had been sent. The few vid records that existed of the attacks were being analyzed and the analyses re-analyzed. Half a dozen theories were posited.

It looked great on the surface, but as Dex dug deeper it was pretty much a load of sound and fury.

Well, it *was* only day one.

DEX REFOCUSSED ON THE physical world, stood and stretched. He left the office and padded to the chiller drawer, trying not to disturb Annabelle. She looked so intent on her work that he bet he could have brought his band through here and she wouldn't have noticed.

That thought gave him pause. It had been months since he and his band Chemical Celeste had played a gig. He wondered if it was even reasonable to call them his band anymore. They'd taken a break when he moved and a couple of the other members had work things going on, and then they'd just never reconnected. This was how it happened, Dex knew. This was how people lost contact, how friendships faded away. He was no stranger to this behaviour, but it wasn't the way he wanted to be anymore.

He grabbed a bottle of water from the chiller and a bag of snax, then went back to the closet office. He thought about all the people he considered friends, but who he hadn't talked to recently. His oldest friend Maks lived half a world away, but that was no impediment when there was M City. Maks's daughter Andrea lived in Dex's own building, but they'd lost touch after the M City crisis was over. Even Zizou's visit to his office had been a surprise, and since then it had been all business.

He wasn't worried that he was returning to the bad old days of being sad and alone, but he had gone back to some bad habits. This was a good opportunity to reach out to those people.

He spent the next two hours sending messages and having chat sessions. By the time he was done, he'd booked a rehearsal for Chemical Celeste, made a date with Maks to get together in M City and obtained several promises to let him know if anyone heard about rogue vigilantes. It felt productive but it also felt good.

He logged back into the M City squad board on the off chance that someone had turned up something new when he noticed a flag from his system. It was low priority and associated with another case, which was why he hadn't seen it until now. He paged over and saw that it was the results of the scan he'd done for chatter about Blockchain. For a second he couldn't even place the name, then remembered that he still technically had an open case — Izzy Marcula.

Most of the talk was marketing bullshit, so he had his system hide those. The rest were mainly glowing testimonials from happy customers, which surprised Dex until he saw the dates — they were all several years old. He reordered the data by most recent and the tenor of the posts changed rapidly. He scanned the complaints until he came across an article that didn't immediately seem to apply here. It was an in-depth analysis of a firm called Endurance and from the stub Dex figured that the analysis was not favourable. He wondered why this post had been flagged, so he paged over and began to read.

Around the time that Blockchain's reputation began to tank, it had been acquired by Endurance, which was no coincidence. Apparently, Endurance's business model was simple — acquire smaller companies in the data block hosting business and then run them into the ground. It appeared to have a double-edged purpose: every small player that was acquired by Endurance further consolidated their position in the hosting market, and many pre-paid customers became so frustrated with the poor performance of their hosting once it was under the Endurance umbrella that they abandoned their contracts. It was money left lying on the table, that Endurance was happy to scoop up as they went by.

Sure, these were small sums, but thousands of small sums added up to a tidy profit, especially when the overhead was essentially zero.

Well, this was a hollow victory. It wasn't even a victory at all, really, except that Dex had solved the mystery. Of course, it wasn't even really much of a mystery that some companies treated their customers like shit. He felt a brief moment of kinship toward the storefront vigilantes, but then tamped down the feeling. He filled out his report for the Marcula case, then sent her his findings along with a recommendation to try fighting for a refund. He wondered if a company whose basic strategy was to screw customers out of what was, for them, small change would bother to work too hard to avoid paying a refund. As Annabelle would put it, the return on investment would start to go down the more effort they'd have to put in to keep the cash.

Well, it was worth a shot, anyway.

ANNABELLE WAS STILL LIGHT years away, so Dex grabbed a quick shower and changed, then headed out of the apartment. He had nowhere to be but it was good to feel the sunlight on his skin and get his legs moving. He aimed himself in the opposite direction from his usual haunts and walked toward the business district. As he got closer, the architecture changed from the unique structures that characterized this Mediterranean city and began to look more like what he'd been accustomed to back in Namerica.

Here were the tall plastiglass and chrome office blocks of the global firms. Dex had spent a few decades working in offices that could be printed copies of these buildings. He watched as individuals in matching uniforms entered and exited one of the towers; rotating shifts kept a staff on at all times. It was a sight as common as dirt — more common, really, if you meant dirt as in soil as opposed to dirt as in dust.

From his perspective now, they reminded him of the bots who had shown him the disk blocks for sale. Their functions were clearly defined, monitored and evaluated. Thanks to their employer-provided uniforms and employer-provided nutritional supplements, they even all looked pretty much the same. Did no one notice how odd it all was?

Now that he was out of the system, it was easy for Dex to look at these people with their mundane work and little room for potential advancement, and think that it was an oppressive regime. But he remembered his own days of shift work, the normalcy that came with living a life that was a copy of everyone you knew. Work, home, inexpensive passive entertainment, sleep, repeat.

The very definition of a normal life.

But why did it have to be that way?

SEVENTEEN

WHEN DEX GOT BACK TO THE APARTMENT Annabelle was done her workday and had already opened a bottle of synthwine.

"Celebrating?"

She grinned. "I finally got to the end of the security patch. I'm down to having one job and it's not even full time."

"Congratulations! You sharing that celebration or should I leave you two alone?" Dex gestured to the bottle condensing in her grip.

"I suppose I could be persuaded to share," she said, getting another glass and pouring out a measure. They clinked glasses and drank.

"So, you're going to have a bit more free time now, I suppose," Dex said.

"Yeah," Annabelle said but she didn't sound entirely certain.

"What?"

"I've... got a line on a few other things," she admitted. "I don't want to get complacent. One completed gig does not a robust resume make."

Dex laughed. "Well, can you at least try not to get another job until you've had a full night's sleep? Maybe even two, if that's not too extravagant."

"I'll try." She gave him a look which implied that he was being overprotective, but Dex could tell that she was running herself down. The dark circles under her eyes didn't make her any less beautiful, but they did worry him.

"So, do you want to tell me how it went?" he asked, sinking into a chair. "Or is it a top secret security patch?"

"Not secret at all," Annabelle said, "but pretty boring. That's the other problem with just starting out — it's not like I can pick and choose the most interesting jobs. This was only a step above what running a script would have been."

Dex doubted that Stella Bish would be wasting Annabelle's talents on a job that could have been automated, but he sympathized with her frustration at its lack of complexity. It was the price of being truly exceptional at what she did.

She took a drink of her wine and sighed. "The only thing that made it at all interesting is that they require their system to be capable of handling anonymous logins, but authenticating each one against itself."

Dex wasn't following at all, and he must have looked it, because Annabelle explained. "So, I want to take a course on whatever it is they teach there. But I don't want to be identified or have any record of it being me who's in attendance. So far, no big deal — being anonymous online isn't hard. But what's harder is having an anonymous account on their system so my attendance, assignments, grades, or whatever are all tied to me, but not tied to my real identity. Does that make sense?"

"I think so," Dex said. "But surely you'd just give everyone a user and pass, and leave it at that? Like an anonymous messenger?"

"Yes and no," Annabelle said. "M City has all those authentication protocols that are tied to our specific systems. That's what makes it hard to create multiple accounts. Obviously, there are ways around that, but usually it's the user who has to make the effort there. Here, they want to handle it all on their end."

"Huh. Is that even possible?"

"Oh, sure," Annabelle said, grinning. "It's just technical and difficult. Lucky for me."

"Well, I can see why Ms. Bish recommended you for that job," Dex said. "That's exactly the kind of thing that's up your street."

"Mhmm." Annabelle's smile faded and she sat her glass down. "It did get me wondering why exactly they're doing it, though. I mean, it's none of my business, and as much as I don't exactly trust Stella Bish, I don't think she'd be involved in something dangerous. But with everything else going on... why the big need for secrecy?"

Dex pondered. "It was a training lab you said?" Annabelle nodded. "But what kind of training..."

"Never came up," she said. "I was up to my ass in the code; I never even saw the rez or the front end."

Dex nodded thoughtfully. "You did get the name of the outfit, though."

"Of course. *Better Biz Brigade*." She snorted. "Pretty cheesy, huh?"

"Yeah," Dex said. "Doesn't give much of an indication about what they do. Maybe some kind of upskilling? But for what?"

"I don't know," Annabelle shrugged.

"Well, it doesn't really matter," Dex said.

"Nope," Annabelle said, biting her lower lip. "I'm, uh, running a search for information about them anyway. Curiosity got to me, I guess. No point in having access to all kinds of back door information if I can't use it once in a while, right?" Her words were confident, but her tone was anything but.

"Feeling guilty about digging into one of your clients?"

"A little. I mean, it's not like I need to know what they do."

"Sure, but I don't think there's anything wrong with wanting to know who's paying your bills."

"I guess." Annabelle finished her wine and slotted the glass into the cleaner. "You mind if I just watch a movie then head to bed? You were right about me needing a decent sleep."

"Sure thing." He leaned over and gave her a kiss. "You want some company for the movie?"

"Seriously?" Annabelle gave Dex a look. "It's one of those dumb actions sims you hate."

"I promise not to make fun of it too loudly," Dex grinned.

"Well, all right. See you in the Roxy, then."

"I'll bring the popcorn," Dex said, and linked into the M City cinema, ordering about half the snack bar and finding Annabelle in one of the couple seats in the back row.

"You'll hold my hand in the scary parts?"

"Shut up and watch the movie," Annabelle said, but she took his hand and held on. And not just for the scary parts.

THE NEXT MORNING WAS a leisurely affair, and Annabelle

didn't even log in to M City until nearly midday. Dex decided that it was time for him to get out of the apartment and get out into the streets. He set off with no particular destination in mind, but then began to think about the events of the last few days. He was reminded of Jamie Eristo's thoughts after the explosion, how angry they had been. Terrorists — that was the word they had used. Dex had thought it was a bit of an overreaction at the time, but now... He wondered if Jamie knew something he didn't.

He pinged Jamie, not expecting a response, but they answered in real time and suggested a meeting. Dex didn't have any other plans, so he suggested the same stim bar when they'd met previously. Jamie had seemed comfortable there, and Dex didn't care one way or another.

When he arrived, Jamie was just settling in to a corner table, a stim bulb in their hand. They lifted their other hand in a greeting and Dex crossed the small space to the table.

"How are things?" he asked as he sat.

"Good. Busy," Jamie answered, taking a hit off the bulb. "Now that we know these storefront attacks are part of something bigger, there's a lot of scrutiny on everything we've already done."

"That's not going to be a problem, is it?" Dex asked, then quickly clammed up as a server approached the table. "Lemon tea?" he asked and the server nodded, waiting for the stim order. "Plain, thanks." The server cocked an eyebrow, but then turned and went back to the bar without commentary.

"No," Jamie said, picking up the conversational thread. "No problem. Just work. Not that I'm complaining. I'll be perfectly happy to see whoever is behind this get what's coming to them. People like this, who assume that just because you have to work for a living that you're part of the system, part of what needs to get broken... I just don't have any time for that."

Dex wasn't entirely certain that he followed where Jamie was going with this line of thought, but he got the gist. Jamie was pissed and wanted to find the group as much as anyone else.

Dex's tea arrived and he took a sip of the steaming liquid. It was surprisingly good. He'd expected a run down stim place to use cheap bases for their cocktails, but he thought there might actually be essence of real fruit in there somewhere.

"Any leads so far?" he asked.

Jamie shook their head. "It's early days, of course. Right now we've been told to look into anything that seems organized, that's counter-culture, that's vocally anti-corporate." They shook their head and took another hit of the stim bulb. The tension in their shoulders visibly reduced and Dex saw a couple of lines in Jamie's face disappear. As much as he didn't enjoy stims, he could appreciate their value.

"I get it," Jamie went on, "it's the obvious thing to look for. It's just that perfectly reasonable people might get caught up in this, people who have nothing to do with these attacks but who are just trying to make things a little bit better..." They seemed to stop themselves from saying more and smiled. "Anyway, you know how it is. You have to chase a few false trails before you find what you're after, right? That's the system, like it or lump it."

Dex nodded, wondering where Jamie's train of thought had been headed before it had been carefully derailed. He couldn't fault them for being circumspect; they'd only met recently and Jamie didn't really know Dex from a hole in the wall. Except...

"So, it's none of my business, but I asked Annabelle about you," Dex said, carefully watching Jamie's face to see if he was putting himself in the soup, but they didn't seem to be upset.

"Yeah. That was a bit awkward, seeing her the other day," Jamie said. "We felt like such good friends, but after the clinic... Honestly, I hadn't really thought about her in years."

"Don't feel bad," Dex smiled. "That's pretty much exactly what she said. I think it was probably one of those circumstantial things — it happens on cases, sometimes, too. You spend a lot of time with someone, in trying conditions, and you become close. Then that circumstance is gone and the friendship fades away. I think it's normal."

Jamie nodded. "Yeah, probably. It was strange to see her again, though. I'm glad she's happy. Especially that you're still in the picture."

"About that..." Dex's stomach knotted and he desperately didn't want ask the question on his mind. He also knew that he couldn't not ask. "I don't want you to break a confidence or anything. But it's been bothering me ever since Annabelle told me she was getting the work done." He took a deep breath and found that he couldn't meet Jamie's eye. "She always said she didn't do it for me, but..."

"Oh." Jamie reached over and brushed Dex's hand, startling him into looking at them. "I can see why you might think that, after what I said the other night. But you should believe her. We talked a lot at the clinic — about our lives before, why we were there... Things you don't tell just anyone, you know? And I can tell you that she was there for no one but herself — to finally feel like she was herself no matter where she was."

Dex nodded, still unsure. Jamie must have sensed his ambivalence, because they added, "I did the get the feeling that being with you gave her something that helped her make the decision. Moral support, or a sense that someone really saw her despite appearances. Or maybe it was simply a kick in the pants, I don't know. Does that make sense?"

There was a painful stinging in Dex's sinuses and he didn't trust himself to speak, so he just nodded. Oh, Annabelle. Dex sometimes forgot that he hadn't been the only one whose world turned upside down when she had come into his life.

He sipped his tea slowly, letting the steam condense on his face until he had to wipe it away with the back of his hand.

EIGHTEEN

"I JUST FEEL AWFUL," ANNABELLE SAID. "I can't believe I might have been helping the very people who have been responsible for everything..." Her voice trailed off and Dex leaned across the virtual sofa to take her in his arms.

"You're way ahead of yourself," he said. "There's so much we don't know. And worst case scenario, if they are the ones behind these attacks, then it will be thanks to you that we catch them."

Her response was incomprehensible, muffled as it was by her face being buried in Dex's chest. Incongruously, Dex wondered what process had done that. Was it Annabelle herself, committed so fully to verisimilitude that even when she was upset she made her avatar sound right for the moment? More likely it was an automated process she'd set up in advance, like her seemingly involuntary facial tics.

More importantly, why was he thinking of that when he ought to be focussed on making her feel better? What was wrong with him? Even though their bodies were simulations, the emotions were all real.

"Come on," he said, carefully pulling away from her. "Let's go over what you've found. Methodically, without assuming anything. If they are involved, we'll need more than your sense of concern to go after them."

"It's more than a sense of concern," she snapped, then took a breath. "Sorry. I know what you mean."

"Okay," Dex said, standing and holding his hand out for her to take. "Let's get cracking."

There was a set of files and charts laid out on the boardroom table in the squad office. Annabelle had copied them to the case file as soon as she realized what they meant.

"So, here is the list of courses available to authenticated users of the *Better Biz Brigade*. It's completely different to the public facing list and look at this: 'Building your own business on the boss's time.' 'Private housing — where to find it and how to pay for it.' These are essentially how-to courses for anti-corporate goons."

"I don't know," Dex said, unsure. "Those look like exactly the kinds of things we do around here."

"Okay, fine," Annabelle said, then riffled thought the files. "Here. What about these?"

Dex read off the items she highlighted. *Spoofing corporate authentication. Creating a local resistance network.* He nodded. Those did look more suspicious. A month ago, he probably wouldn't have given them a second thought. He might even have filed the lab away as a potential resource. But now...

"Okay, this does look bad," he said. "I'm going to let the captains know about this, see if we can get some more information about what they really do over there."

Annabelle nodded, still looking sick.

"You didn't do anything wrong," Dex said. "You know that, right?"

She nodded, but he wasn't convinced.

"Look, this whole thing is complicated. I get why these people want to do something to take the firms down a notch. Things have gotten a lot worse in the last few years, and if we just lie down and let it happen, it will get worse still. I can sympathize with the tactics this group is using, even while I know we need to find them and stop them."

He picked up one of the files, an encrypted listing of the training site's member list. "Even if the people at *Better Biz Brigade* are part of this, that doesn't exactly make them the bad guys. Depending on how they're involved it might not make them bad guys at all. And whatever their involvement, you doing a little job for them definitely doesn't make you a bad guy, okay?"

"Yeah, okay, you're right," Annabelle said. "It was just a bit of a surprise, you know? And not in a good way."

"Yeah, I know," Dex said. "But look at it another way — this is the first actual lead we've had. And it wouldn't have happened if you didn't take that job."

"Yeah, yeah, I'm a goddamn hero," Annabelle said bitterly, but she smiled. That was good enough for Dex.

AFTER ANNABELLE LINKED OUT of the squad room to get back to her rez job, Dex finished off his report. He found that he was in two minds — from one perspective, he wanted to put a stop to these attacks as soon as possible. If BBB was a real lead in that direction, it could bust this case wide open. But even now he felt like what BBB was trying to do was fundamentally no different from what he and Annabelle and the rest of them were doing. Trying to carve a slice of life away from being dependent on some faceless HR department, and helping other people do the same.

He refused to believe that wanting something more was wrong. He refused to condemn the idea of helping other people get a taste of the freedom he already enjoyed.

He knew that the difference between what he was comfortable with and what the storefront attackers were doing was only a matter of details and degrees. But he also believed that those details mattered. So he had to find out exactly what BBB was doing.

And what better way than to sign up and take a course?

DEX LINKED OVER TO his office to have a think and to get away from the shiny, clean brightness of the squad offices. He leaned back in his chair, feet on his desk and pulled his hat down low over his eyes. He could still see perfectly well but it felt like a good thinking position.

He knew he could sign up for a benign-sounding course at BBB, take it, then another, and methodically work his way into their confidences. It would be the best way, of that there was no doubt. But it would be slow and take time away from the rest of his work and if he were being completely honest with himself, he just wasn't willing to wait.

Usually he was a reasonably patient person, especially when it came to work. He liked to let a puzzle work itself out in his subconscious, and found that trying to rush a solution usually ended up costing more time in the end. But this was different — it wasn't figuring out a puzzle, it was getting information. And Dex knew that if what you wanted could be found in files online, there were shortcuts to getting it.

Annabelle could crack their security in her sleep. She could have even before she got firsthand experience with their system. But she hadn't mentioned that, even when she was still in the throes of her guilt trip. It didn't mean she wouldn't do it, but it did mean that it wasn't her first thought. And Dex didn't love the idea, either. If BBB wasn't involved in these storefront attacks, breaking into their system would compromise a lot of people who obviously valued anonymity. No, there had to be another way.

He was letting that puzzle play out in the back of his mind when his system prodded him with a notification. He knocked his hat back on his head and sat up. A vague glow emanated from his inbox and Dex pulled the file folder to his green felt blotter. He flipped it open — it was the analysis he'd run on the Oyuba tenants of the disk blocks which were listed for sale. It had completed days ago, but he'd dismissed the notification and then forgotten about it. Luckily, his system knew him, and popped the notification back up after the file had remained unopened for a while.

He scanned the results and immediately saw that there was something odd going on at Oyuba. All the disk blocks which were now for sale had gone through a series of owners in the past several years. The same series of owners, all originating in being owned by an arm of Oyuba. Dex did a quick lookup of the other hosts, and until the two most recent owners, they were all sub-brands of Oyuba. Then all the blocks transferred ownership to a small private company called Colex, which seemed to be a black hole of information. They had no existing online presence, they appeared to no longer have any holdings, and any historical information simply led back to a set of disk blocks. A set of twelve disk blocks — exactly the number that Irina Nightingale bequeathed to whoever she bequeathed them to.

Dex was fairly certain that Irina Nightingale was Colex, or maybe it was more like the other way around. Private owners weren't listed by name, so each disk block could theoretically have passed through several private owners before it got to Nightingale, but Dex doubted it. Checking the dates, Colex appeared to have dissolved only about a month before Irina Nightingale died and all these disk blocks became part of her estate. Before she posthumously distributed them to other individuals.

What was she up to? And how did she manage to take over a significant fraction of a big firm's disk block business, essentially without anyone noticing?

DEX LINKED OUT OF his office and refocussed on the physical world. His head was toying with the idea of aching and something felt strange in his belly. Oh yeah, hunger. He wondered how much time he'd spent in M City in the last 48 hours — more than usual, he was sure. He padded out of the closet office and grabbed something for his rumbling gut. He poked around in Annabelle's stim cupboard, looking for something for his head, but after finding half a dozen items with baffling names and combinations of effect, he gave up. He always felt weird on stims anyway, and he was probably just dehydrated.

He grabbed a bottle of water and downed it before realizing that Annabelle wasn't there. There was a note icon blinking on their tabletop, so he tapped it open.

"Had an idea. Gone to the beach. Ping me. <3"

That was odd, but the beach was one of the few places in the physical world that Annabelle enjoyed. Maybe Dex's weird ways were rubbing off on her. Still — it kind of gave him the creeps.

He popped another bottle of water and sat at the table. As much as he wanted to run after Annabelle, she was an adult. If she wanted to feel the sand between her toes, then she could go and do that and she didn't need him hovering over her to make sure she was okay. She'd lived here without him for a long time. He needed to stop being so protective. The timestamp on the note meant that she wouldn't have left the apartment more than half an hour previously. He'd give her some time before he butted in.

In order to stop himself from watching the minutes take their interminable time ticking over, Dex logged in to the local squad board. He hadn't checked it in days and he was somehow surprised to see that the storefront attacks had continued. There had been the usual several days grace period, when the local team was off busting up shops in some neighbouring town no doubt, but yesterday there had been another attack that followed the pattern precisely. A 24-hour stim kiosk down by the entertainment district was vandalized when the clerk closed briefly to attend to a personal emergency. Toilet break, Dex figured, but that was a costly time to be caught out. The clerk had been dismissed on the spot.

Fuck. What was wrong with these people? How could they not see that a bit of broken plastiglass and some wrecked stock wasn't going faze an outfit like Empyre? But this clerk — where were they going to go now? Would this be one more person living in a makeshift shanty on the beach?

The beach. Dammit, Dex didn't care any more if he was

getting in her way, he wanted to know what could possibly have prompted Annabelle to go for an honest to god walk. He pinged her and found his fingers drumming incessantly on the tabletop as he waited for an answer. Finally, he heard her voice.

"Hey, Dex!"

"You okay?"

She laughed. "Of course. But, if you're free, you might want to join me. I've been talking with some people you might like to meet."

NINETEEN

EVEN THOUGH SHE'D MADE IT a good way down the beach toward the airport, it didn't take long for Dex to find Annabelle. She was the one with half a dozen rough-looking streeters sitting in front of her.

As he was approaching, he pinged her again. "Everything okay?"

"Yeah," she answered, "I am capable of having a conversation with people out here, you know."

He was chastened, but then she went on. "I'll be glad when you get here, though. I'm about ready to be done."

He picked up the pace, even though walking in sand always made him feel like he was on a treadmill.

People routinely went out of their way to avoid streeters. There were stories about them attacking folks, but in Dex's experience they were no more likely to be dangerous than anyone else. He figured the real reason was that no one liked to be reminded of the realities of poverty. Of how close most of them were to being in the same position as that person living out of a bag.

Dex took a breath to fortify himself as he approached the

group. He wasn't immune to those feelings, he just knew what they were. It only made it easier — it didn't make it easy.

"Hi," Annabelle said as he grew near. To the group she said, "This is Dex. We work together." The odd emphasis she put on the word "work" meant that she must have identified herself as a member of the nameless security organization. That they both operated out of M City didn't change the fact that these people would recognize them as being, at least, not a threat. Hopefully, as allies.

"This is Kristal," Annabelle said, gesturing toward a dark-skinned woman wearing what looked like a corporate uniform with the emblems removed. She was the least scruffy-looking of the group and could have passed for someone's employee if one didn't look too closely. "She's been telling me about some people we probably ought to get to know."

Dex gave Annabelle the side eye and she responded with a raised eyebrow and a sweet smile. Dex had no idea what that meant.

"I'm really surprised you don't know about these guys," Krystal said. "I figured they were part of your outfit. Or at least adjacent to it, you know?"

"I'm sorry," Dex said, "but you have me at an advantage. What guys?"

The small man next to Kristal barked a laugh. "They aren't like a social club or something. I don't think they have a name. It's just folks."

Dex made a face but kept quiet, waiting for someone to start providing actual details. He had enough experience with situations like this to know that letting the conversation unfold at it own pace was more likely to be productive than trying to steer it. People liked to tell their stories their own way.

"That's true," Kristal said. "But there is some kind of organization. A bunch of people doing random stuff on their own couldn't have done this." She spread her arms to encompass the jury rigged dwellings up past the high tide mark.

Things started to drop into place for Dex. He now saw that each shelter, while uniquely homebrew on the outside, had several aspects in common. Each one seemed to have a portable sanitary unit and there was a small combination zapper/chiller, and a few had external everywherenet interfaces. Dex hadn't met many people who hadn't had the implants installed either at school or work, but there were some. And obviously, those people would be more likely to be streeters.

"This is some kind of..." Dex searched for the correct anachronistic terminology. "Humanitarian aid."

Annabelle nodded.

"It's not a free hand out," the man said, indignant. "We're expected to pay it on to the next person who ends up down here with nothing. And we do. We've figured out that we can do a lot better if we stick together." He angled his head toward what Dex thought was a particularly large shelter, maybe for a couple, but now saw was a community space. There were secured storage units, a large chiller and what Dex thought might be a full-sized shower.

"It's almost like an open air dorm," he said, then immediately wished he could take it back. There might be the most rudimentary comforts here, but these were still barely shelters. "I'm sorry," he said, looking at each one of them. "I don't mean to make light of your situation."

"It's all right," the man said. "I think we all knew what

you meant."

One of the people near the end said in a quiet voice, "I lived in a dorm once that was worse than this. At least we have hot water." There were a few nods but Dex still felt like an asshole.

"Do you have any idea where they get their supplies?" Annabelle asked, bringing the conversation back.

Kristal shook her head. "I have a contact — it's an anonymous messenger, but it's always the same person who comes. We let them know what we need and sometimes we get it, sometimes we don't."

"Don't get the wrong idea," the man said, "these people aren't just throwing euros at us. The chillers and lavs are only a small part of what they provide. The real asset they've shared with us is information."

Dex felt Annabelle tense and he looked over. It didn't look like fear or discomfort, more like anticipation.

"What kind of information?"

"Ways to get a currency account without a job," Kristal said, "places to find cheap or free clothes, how to start a business online, the whole gamut. Everything from basic how-not-to-starve tips for folks who are new to the streets, to ways to build a full life outside of having a corporate job." She shrugged. "There's even a whole course on how to get into a corporate job if that's the route a person wants to go."

"Wait," Dex said, "a *course*? This is a school?"

Annabelle grinned now. "Dex, meet some of the graduates of *Better Biz Brigade*."

"JUST BECAUSE THEY ARE doing some good things, that

doesn't mean that they aren't involved in the attacks." Dex had been impressed with the things the group on the beach had told them, but he was even more suspicious of BBB now. They obviously had an agenda, and it was easy to see how a path could be traced between helping victims of corporate insensitivity to starting a more active fight.

"I know," Annabelle said, "that's why I asked you to join us. I get the impression that if there is a connection, it's not all the way though the training organization. First off, we think these attacks are being perpetrated by only two or three people per area. From what Kristal told me, there are dozens of people involved in Nice alone. And BBB has likely been training people all around the world."

Dex nodded. "I bet it's one of those situations where the right hand doesn't know what the left hand is doing."

"Or, to make a mess of your body part metaphor, that the left hand pinkie finger is off doing its own operation which it thinks is in keeping with the rest of the body's ideals, but really is just causing more trouble."

"That... isn't really how metaphors work," Dex said, a grin sneaking on to his face.

"You knew what I meant," Annabelle said with mock outrage.

"Anyway, how are we going to find out what those hands and fingers really are doing?" he asked. "I'm not willing to put in the months it would take to become a trusted member of their community in the hopes that we might come across some useful tidbit."

"I think I might have a way to skip ahead a little bit." Annabelle winked and sent Dex a link.

Curious, he followed it to a text-only workspace. It was familiar; Annabelle often wrote code without any kind graphical interface and she'd shown him things like this before, but he'd never understood what he was looking at. Now was no different.

"This is a mockup of the user administration code they use at BBB," Annabelle said. "I put this together from memory, so it's not functional in any way, but you get the idea. This here—" a string of text near the top became highlighted in gold, "is a brand new user account. This value here—" the highlighting condensed to show the number #000, "indicates its level. Brand new is zero, each course increments it by one or maybe more depending on the course type. There might be other ways that the level changes, the methodology doesn't really matter to us. What matters to us is figuring out what that value needs to be in order to get access to the interesting stuff."

"Okay," Dex said, "I think I get what you're saying. But even if we knew that it takes Level 34 to get the keys to the inner garden, I'm not sure how that helps us?"

"Well, then I'd know what kind of user account to inject into their system," Annabelle said.

Dex felt dumb for not getting where she was going until now. "You're going to make a fake user."

"Well, it wouldn't be a completely fake user," Annabelle said. "It would really be you or me or Ruby — whoever. Just a fake level value. Call it a kind of advanced placement system."

"That's great. Now, can I get out of this vortex of text, please?"

"Sure," Annabelle laughed. "I forget how disoriented you get in the command line."

Dex grunted and refocussed on their apartment. "You're okay with this?" he asked.

"It's cheating," she admitted. "And if it turns out that we

get information that we end up using, and it comes out that this is how we got it, well, I guess it's safe to say that I'm not going to get a glowing reference from BBB."

"That's a bit of an understatement," Dex said. "Using the knowledge you got working on their systems to essentially crack it..." He drew a sharp intake of breath. "They would have to end up being pretty damned dirty in order for folks to forgive that."

"I know," Annabelle said. "That's why I'm not using anything I learned. The user level is encoded in each user file, so anyone with skill who signed up for a class could see that it was there. The means to inject the, ah, free upgrade is a known exploit. No one cares because it generally has little value."

"I thought you were applying a security patch to their system, though."

"I was," Annabelle said, "but not that one."

"Seriously?"

"People think that systems are locked down like a vault, but just like everything else in the world it's all trade-offs. The systems that take care of currency accounts, those are tight. The database that remembers your drinks order," she shrugged. "Not so much."

"But surely BBB would treat their user account database as a secure asset."

"As a whole, sure, but each constituent part has its own protections. It's complicated, and I doubt you really want the two hour explanation, but the long and short of it is I can upgrade a user to look like a trusted, authenticated member. It's not root access or anything close to it, but we ought to be able to find out what's really going on at BBB."

"I don't know," Dex said, "I don't want to put you in a bad

position. Especially on a wild goose chase."

"Damn it, Dex, this was my idea. If I want to jeopardize my freelance career, that's my choice. I don't think it's going to come to that. And at the moment, I don't see any other way to get what we need. Does anyone else have any great ideas for finding who's responsible? Anything that even smells like a lead? No? Well, okay, then."

Dex wasn't about to change her mind. He wondered how much of this was her trying to atone for possibly working with an organization that was responsible for the attacks. And, if he were honest with himself, he knew that if there weren't any potential personal repercussions for her he wouldn't have any problem with this plan at all. He was being overprotective and it wasn't fair.

But he couldn't help the way it made his stomach knot.

"Okay," he conceded. "Do you just do your magic now or what?"

"No, create the account the regular way first," she said. "Like I said, it's not a fake account. This is almost entirely aboveboard."

"Yeah, almost," Dex muttered, but she didn't hear. Or at least, she didn't acknowledge it if she did hear. Which was probably for the best.

TWENTY

IT WAS LIKE SOMEONE HAD TAKEN A VID of the meeting a few weeks before — Dex, Susana Bells and Captains Zhang, Biagini and Larsen all sat around the big boardroom table in the squad offices, in exactly the same places they'd been before. Old habits. This time, though, there were no charts or files piled in the centre of the table, and Annabelle had joined them. He supposed that he could have done this in a report, but Dex felt like it deserved a face to face. At least, avatar to avatar.

"You know that I've been spending a lot of time in the social spaces for trainees at *Better Biz Brigade*, hoping to see if anyone there has any connection to or information on whoever is instigating these storefront attacks."

There were nods around the table, some a bit more impatient than others. "Before anyone gets their hopes up too much, I've found no direct evidence that points to any individual or group being involved in the attacks." Someone groaned, but Dex went on before anyone could add voice to complaint. "However, I am convinced we are on the right track. BBB is, without a doubt, a meeting point and training ground for people who are engaged in direct resistance to the firms."

"What do you mean, *resistance?*" That was Susana Bells.

"That's the word they use," Dex explained. "The firms are, of course, motivated by profit, and the path to greater profit often goes against the best interest of the people who generate it — employees and consumers. The people at BBB are trying to push back against the aspects of the system that hurt the people at the bottom."

"So they're revolutionaries," Biagini said, almost approvingly.

Dex shrugged. "Maybe. Most of the people I've talked to don't think of what they are doing as trying to overthrow the economic system we have, exactly. More like... augment it."

Annabelle broke in. "It's very much in the same vein as what we are doing with keeping M City accessible and decentralized. But their focus is in the physical world."

"So, if you think these are the good guys, how are they going to help our investigation?" Larsen asked.

"I think BBB as an organization is working for the kind of changes we'd all support. But as an organization, it's mostly a set of canned course material, a user database and meeting space. It's in that meeting space where the real business is getting done, and that's just folks. Folks who all have their own opinions and perspectives on things. It's not a monolith. And it's also not that small."

Dex pulled up a chart of anonymous users divided by geographical login area. "Of course, we all know there are lots of ways to spoof your location, and I have no doubt whatsoever that some not small percentage of the BBB userbase employs those tools on the regular. But putting that aside for a moment, you can see that BBB has logins from everywhere." Dex had the chart redeploy its data to show a world map with logins highlighted. There were no landmasses unrepresented and a few dots even appeared offshore.

"Because logins are anonymized, and people come and go, there's no way to know how many people are currently active. Also, each user's level of involvement is highly variable — one person might sign up for a single course and that's the end of it. Someone else might share their login with a friend, while another uses the meeting space as their primary social life. But, best guess, there are thousands of people from all over who are actively involved in some level of street action, organized via BBB."

Dex paused to let everyone digest the information.

"So, what's your next step?" Captain Zhang asked.

"I've gotten friendly with a group that's local to me. They have been helping to set up a kind of streeter community with basic supplies and information. Everything I've heard about what they do sounds like they're perfectly reasonable, but there have also been some conversations on the boards that are..." Dex thought for the right word. "More extreme. Definitely on the revolutionary side of things."

"Like what?"

"Like debating how it might be possible to hold a firm accountable for firing someone without cause. Like discussion about whether it's acceptable to appropriate personal items supplied through employment once that employment ends."

"You mean stealing."

Dex shrugged. "I'd say so. Others in the group argue that it's stealing for the firm to demand the return of those items. Anyway, we don't need to have the debate, I'm just letting you know the kind of ideas being thrown around. Which makes me wonder if some of these people might know of anyone who is taking matters into their own hands."

"Or maybe doing it themselves," Zhang said.

"Exactly. It's a long shot, but it's the only shot we have. So I'm going to be joining up with their physical world group tomorrow."

"Is that safe?" Larsen asked.

"I can't see why not," Dex said. "I'm already a part of their group in the online space. They trust me. And as I said, there's nothing that they are doing that I can't support. All the red flags are just from talk. And there's nothing wrong with talk."

"Well, it's your call," Larsen said. "This meeting isn't in some broken down old warehouse in the back of beyond at 2 am, and also, come alone?"

Dex laughed. "Nope. It's in a public square in the middle of the afternoon. Seriously, even if these people are the ones doing the attacks, I don't think they are dangerous. Misguided, maybe, but even the ones with the most out there views are trying to create a better world. I'm sure of that."

Dex got Larsen to reluctantly agree and the meeting broke up. Before she could leave, Dex cornered Zahara Zhang.

"Got a minute?"

"Sure," she said.

"See you in my office in five?" She nodded and linked out of the boardroom.

"DOES ANY OF THIS mean anything to you?" Dex asked after explaining what he'd found about Oyuba, Colex and Irina Nightingale.

Zhang frowned. "I apprenticed at a company that was a

subsidiary of Oyuba," she said. "But it wasn't Colex." She flipped thought the papers. "I'd left that job long before Colex was even spun out. It was a long time ago, Dex, and I wasn't there very long. You know how it goes."

Dex nodded. "Apprenticeship? You'd have been living in a company dorm, then, right?"

"Sure." She smiled knowingly. "I see where you're going but I can't say I'd have made a strong impression on anyone there. I kept myself to myself back then. I don't even remember the names of my roommates. It was a long time ago."

"What about later?" Dex asked. "Ever have a case involving Oyuba or someone who worked there?"

Zhang frowned. "I can't recall anything off the top of my head. I'll check the files. You think that Nightingale was involved with Oyuba and that's how she knew who I am?"

Dex shrugged. "I don't really think anything yet, but this is what there is to go on. My best guess at the moment is that Nightingale somehow parlayed Colex into her own personal empire. Whether she bought it out, embezzled it, outright stole it — I don't know. But Colex became Nightingale right around here." Dex pointed to some data. "And then she died, and all those Colex holdings got distributed in her will." He made a *poof* gesture with his fingers. "Within just a few years, Nightingale managed to take a small chunk of Oyuba and spread it around a bunch of people who, frankly, would be unlikely to ever own even a timeshare of a single rez space in a disk block."

Zhang's avatar was quiet and still, and Dex recognized that as her thinking. She rarely rushed to a conclusion — it made her a good captain, if sometimes a frustrating one.

"Redistributing wealth from the firms to the regular

folks," she said, almost to herself. "Does that sound familiar?"

"Yeah," Dex said, sinking into his chair. "It does."

"Do I need to be concerned that Oyuba is going to come after me?" Dex knew she wasn't really asking him, rather she was spitballing ideas as they occurred to her. He answered anyway.

"I don't think so. According to everything here, no matter how she actually accomplished it, the data trail is a hundred percent by the book. At the end if the day, those disk blocks were legitimately Nightingale's to give, so now the one you have is legitimately yours."

Zhang nodded absently, her thoughts obviously still racing. "You did some good digging here, Dex," she said. "I knew I could count on you. Trouble is, now I just have more questions."

Dex smiled wryly. "There's a reason we're called investigator, not solvers. There's no guarantee we'll ever get to the bottom of it."

"I know," Zhang said. "Doesn't mean I have to like it."

"Amen to that."

DEX HAD CHANGED HIS outfit four times before Annabelle finally stopped him.

"You look fine," she said, exasperated. "It's not like this is a date."

"What if they can tell I'm not, you now, one of them?" he asked. "Does this shirt make me look like a narc?"

Annabelle laughed. "I think so long as you're not wearing a manager's uniform, you'll be fine. Some of these people are probably going to be streeters. No one is going to notice what you're wearing."

Dex unfastened the dark, silky shirt he was wearing and let it fall off his body. "This is way too expensive! Where's all that stuff I brought with me when I first got here."

Annabelle sighed. She'd taken him shopping after he'd moved to Nice and replaced most of his clothes. He'd just left a corporate job, so didn't have a lot to replace since he'd had to turn in his uniforms.

"How about this?" He held up a vaguely stained, dark brown shapeless top.

"Well, no one could argue that it's too fancy, I'll give you that."

"Good." He put it on and smoothed it over his flat belly. "Still fits."

Annabelle rolled her eyes, but she was smiling. "It's going to be fine. You said it this morning — there's nothing to worry about here."

Dex grunted. "Well, it was easier to say this morning. It's been a while since I've been undercover. Even longer since I've been undercover out here."

Annabelle took his hand. "You're a natural, honey. You're going to do fine. Worst case scenario, ping me and I'll send in the cavalry."

"What cavalry?"

"I'll get René to turn up. He's always good for a disturbance."

That made Dex laugh and he kissed Annabelle before heading for the door.

"If you haven't heard from me in three hours…"

"I know," Annabelle said. "I'll send a search party. Good luck."

"Thanks, kiddo," Dex said and stepped on to the lift.

BY THE TIME HE ARRIVED at the park, he'd walked off his nervousness. Now he was more keyed up by the prospect of learning something about the group. Even if they couldn't lead him to whoever was behind the attacks, he was curious. When he really thought about it, he almost wished that they wouldn't have a connection. He'd become interested in the work they were doing — he could even imagine himself joining them for real.

He was expecting a group of five people, gathered around the statue. He saw a small group waiting and took a deep breath. He wandered over, not wanting to look too eager, when he noticed someone familiar.

Oh, shit. It was Jamie Eristo. They were walking along the path, directly between Dex and the group. Any minute now, they could turn and see him and completely blow the operation. Dex veered to the right to try and get out of Jamie's line of sight but it was too late.

"Dex!" Jamie called loudly, an arm upraised in greeting. "I'm surprised to see it's you, but maybe I shouldn't have been."

Dex found himself rooted to the spot by a combination of confusion and surprise. He still hadn't gotten his head around the situation when Jamie reached him.

"Sorry," they said, "you must be thrown. I'm User647-B. You must be 428-C."

Dex was still at a loss for words, but Jamie took him by the arm and steered him toward the group by the statue.

"Let me introduce you to the rest of the Nice branch of BBB."

Twenty-One

JAMIE INTRODUCED DEX to the other four people, preserving his anonymity, and they talked about what the team had been doing. Dex paid enough attention to answer their questions coherently and make the appropriate noises, but internally he was screaming. He'd set his system to record the meeting of course, his now-lapsed habit of lifelogging pressed into service, which was imperative since almost all he could focus on what figuring out what this meant.

Was his cover blown? He thought the details of this operation had been kept between the people in the previous day's meeting, but they had never actually discussed that. For all he knew, Biagini had passed on the plan to his squad.

And Biagini! Surely he didn't know that one of his officers was involved in this group. What would this mean for Jamie's future? What did it mean for the cases they'd worked on? Was Jamie actually feeding the attackers information about the investigation? Was that why the squad had never been able to find anything?

Dex's mind was in an uproar, and it took all his control just to maintain his composure. He must have pulled it off, though, because after an hour of talking, the tall Asian woman who seemed to be the unofficial leader asked if Dex would be available to help distribute some supplies in Saint-Sylvestre.

"Sure," he answered, hoping that he hadn't agreed to something he'd regret. He needed to review the recording — he could barely remember the details of anything they'd discussed.

"Wonderful," she said. "We'll be in touch through secure message. It will be really great to have another body to help out. There's so much more we'd like to do."

"Absolutely." Dex just wanted to get out of there. "Talk to you soon."

He begged off when Jamie asked if he'd like to get a drink and hoped he hadn't seemed too suspicious. Of course, this whole business was suspicious, but now he was getting paranoid. He needed to get home.

He managed to be deliberately casual in his walk back to the apartment, on the off chance he was being followed. He took the most direct route, but was sure not to hurry. He wanted to look like he had somewhere to be but he didn't want to look like he was panicking. Which he wasn't, but it was close.

The fifteen-minute walk home felt like it took an hour but passed by in a blur. When he fell in the door, Annabelle looked up, worry creased across her face.

"What happened?" She jumped up and came over to Dex, her hand hovering next to his cheek, not quite touching him. "Are you hurt?"

He shook his head. "It's Jamie," he said.

"Jamie Eristo?"

He nodded. "They're part of it."

THE TWO OF THEM WENT over the vid in real time, and every minute that he watched it, Dex calmed a little more. Not only had he comported himself perfectly well, the conversation made the group look like the benign entity Dex hoped it was. But with his identity known, there was no chance of getting anyone to admit to anything now.

"We have to let the captains know about this," Annabelle said. "René... I don't know how he's going to take this."

"If the group is really only up to what they say they are, there's no problem," Dex said. "There's nothing inherently wrong with the operations they have planned or anything else I've seen from these people. Jamie has no reason to think they'd be in trouble for participating."

"So then why didn't they ever mention it?"

"Why would they? They wouldn't have known about our interest in BBB — if they aren't connected to the attacks, there's no reason to bring it up."

Annabelle frowned. "Yeah, you're right. It's easy to forget that we've been working on this lead in isolation. Jamie wouldn't have a clue. But what if they *are* connected, Dex? What if Jamie is..." She didn't finish the thought aloud but Dex knew she was asking herself the same questions he had when he'd first realized his colleague was part of the group.

"We'll just have to cross that bridge if we come to it," he said. "That said, I find it hard to believe that Jamie could be willingly involved. I mean, you should hear them talk about these attacks. They were using words like terrorism — at the time, I sounded more like an apologist for the attackers."

"It could have been a front. They protest too much, maybe?"

"Sure," Dex said reluctantly, not liking the feeling that Jamie had been playing him all along. "Anything is possible."

"If they are involved in the attacks," Annabelle said, "we've just made it a whole lot harder on ourselves."

"I know." Dex rubbed his hands over his face, as if trying to wash away the dual senses of betrayal — both that Jamie might be lying to him and that he might be falsely suspecting Jamie of something they would never do.

"SO WHAT ARE YOUR NEXT STEPS?"

Captain Larsen had taken charge of the meeting after Dex passed on the vid and made a cursory report. René Biagini had taken the news without comment and his avatar didn't give anything away either. Dex was desperate to learn what his old friend thought, but now wasn't the time.

"I'm going to carry on as planned," Dex said. "I'll do this Saint-Sylvestre delivery, learn what I can."

"Surely no one is going to reveal their part in the attacks to you, knowing who... what you are." Larsen's usually disturbingly genial face was deformed by a scowl.

"They don't necessarily know," Annabelle said. "There's no indication that Jamie has mentioned their work to the group." Larsen grunted but didn't offer a rebuttal.

"And, of course, there isn't necessarily anything for anyone to reveal," Captain Zhang said. "This whole operation was a stab in the dark, let's not forget that. It's better than even odds that there's nothing here to find."

"You can't prove a negative," Larsen grumped. "This is a waste of time."

"Maybe," Dex said. "But worst case scenario: they know something, but no one tells me. Maybe they'll get scared off because we're getting close and attacks stop. That's fine with me. Even if nothing changes, we're still in the same position we'd been in before."

"Do we really want *another* one of our officers connected with this... group?" Larsen spat out the final word and shot Biagini a glare.

"Why not?" René said. "As far as we know, they are doing good work. It's about time we looked beyond these walls of pixels and light and started helping people out there as well as in here."

"And if their idea of 'fighting the good fight' involves vandalism and sabotage? Are you good with that?"

"Of course not," Biagini snapped. "But if it doesn't, and they're out there putting action to their words and truly helping people, should we be blocking that? Should I censure one of my officers because they're putting in their own time to help make things better? Should we let the people this group is helping continue to suffer because we've got no other leads?" He turned to look directly at Larsen. "Are *you* good with *that*?"

"Enough," Zhang said. "Let's see what this meeting brings. Dex, when are you joining them for deliveries?"

"I haven't heard yet," he said, "but it should be in the next few days."

"Right," she said, standing. "There's nothing more to do about it now. Let's reconvene after this delivery and figure out what, if anything, we should do at that time. Sound reasonable, Captains?" She looked from Biagini to Larsen, the expression on her avatar's face almost daring them to argue.

Neither of them took the bait.

"WELL, THAT WAS UNPLEASANT." Dex gnawed at a food brick and rummaged in the chiller. Nothing in there seemed appealing. He wanted a drink — a real drink in a real bar, but he wanted to be with Annabelle more.

"Yes, it was, " Annabelle answered. "You look kind of restless. You need to get out for a bit?"

"No, I'm fine." Dex paced the small space between the chiller and the door to the apartment, back and forth, back and forth. At one of his apogees, Annabelle stood and went into the bedroom. He heard her in the closet then the sounds of clothes falling. On his next pass by the door he peeked in and saw she'd changed into a nice sundress. It was one of his favourites.

"You're not going out like that," she said when she returned to the main room, eyeing his perfectly serviceable outfit. He looked down.

"I guess not?" She nodded once and moved so he could get into the bedroom. He found a sleeveless top and a pair of slim fitting trousers laid out for him. "I can take a hint."

When he'd changed, they spiralled down the lift and headed out into the mid-afternoon sun.

"You up for Le Rétro?" Dex asked, already turning in that direction.

"I wouldn't be here if I wasn't."

The walk was pleasant as always, though Dex found his attention being drawn to the rough-looking people they passed. How many of them were the beneficiaries of BBB's operations? Alternatively, how many were the victims of the aftermath of one of the storefront attacks?

"It's not black and white," Annabelle said, obviously having similar thoughts. "Hardly anything we do is; I think I just like to tell myself I know we're doing the right thing because if I really thought about it every time I crack into a database or send the goon squad to hassle some dirtbag, well..."

"Yeah," Dex agreed. "We'd never do anything."

"All those people, the ones we stop from hassling folks or shaking down some online artist — they're the heroes of their own story."

"That might be going too far." Dex shot her a look.

"Who knows why people do what they do? When you've been shit on by the world, it's easy to feel like someone else owes you something. Maybe you can't go after the people who hurt you or someone else who deserves it, but there's someone you can kick. Someone you can tell yourself is just a tool of the system, who probably would do the same thing themselves in your place. It's rationalizing the choice you were going to make all along. It's what we do, why not them, too?"

"Jesus, Annabelle."

"I know, I know," she said, squeezing his hand. "Moral relativity only goes so far. Just... sometimes it's easy to forget that there's lots of different ways to look at things. And who's in the right and who's not isn't always so clear."

Dex nodded, glad that the familiar faded red awning of Le Rétro had appeared around the corner. "Come on, let's deal with this deep philosophical debate in the time honoured tradition." He stepped through the open façade of the building and into the relative gloom of the bar.

It was late enough in the day that many of the tables were taken, but there were still a few spots to choose from. Dex scanned the room, looking for a place where Annabelle would be most comfortable. He saw a table in a corner, where one of the seats had two walls in behind. He gestured toward it and

Annabelle nodded.

"I'll grab our drinks from the bar," Dex said. "What can I get you?"

"Just a fancy water is good."

Dex found a spot at the busy bar and grabbed one of the tablet menus rather than wait for the human bartender. He punched in an order for a bubbly water with lemon for Annabelle and splurged on a Caña and water for himself. A large. He found their table on the map to finish the order, then scanned the chip in his hand to pay. It was impersonal but efficient.

When he got to the table, Annabelle had a look on her face.

"What's up?"

She shushed him impatiently and gestured for him to sit. "Did they see you?"

He began to turn to look at the rest of the bar, but she stopped him.

"Who?"

"René is at the other side of the bar," she hissed, "with Jamie."

TWENTY-TWO

"WHAT ARE THEY DOING? WHAT CAN YOU SEE? Are they fighting? What's happening?"

"I can't tell," Annabelle said, her voice hushed as if they could hear her all the way across the crowded bar.

"One bubbly water and one rum?" A server appeared with their drinks, placing them on the table.

"Thanks," Dex said, taking the opportunity to sneak a peek across the bar. It was definitely René and Jamie, but in the second's glance he got he couldn't tell anything.

"I've got an idea," Annabelle said. "Hang on." She blinked unnaturally a few times and then got the far-off stare of someone online. Dex got a ping on his system and blinked over to see a link to a live vid feed.

"You're brilliant," he said as he joined the feed, now seeing what Annabelle saw. His own face staring back at him was unnerving for a moment, but her attention soon shifted back to René and Jamie. She fiddled with the settings and soon they were in sharper focus.

There was no way to tell what they were saying, but their facial expressions were clear. René didn't look like his usual gregarious self, but neither did he have the expression of a superior reprimanding subordinate. And Jamie was the one doing most of the talking.

"I wish I learned how to lipread," Annabelle said.

They watched for maybe another minute, when Jamie stood from the table and reached out toward René. Dex tensed, but nothing happened except a short handshake and then Jamie left.

Dex broke the video link and stood. "I'm going over there."

"No—" But he was already halfway across the bar.

"René."

Biagini turned to the sound of Dex's voice with a look of surprise, which quickly turned to a smile.

"Dex! I didn't think I'd be seeing you again so soon. What brings you—"

"I saw you talking with Jamie Eristo." Dex sat, uninvited, in the chart vacated by Jamie.

René nodded, the smile fading. "Jamie is my responsibility."

Dex sat there, unsure what to say. "And?"

René shrugged, his typical insouciance showing through. "And I asked them if they or anyone they knew has anything to do with the attacks."

"You've got to be kidding!" Dex forced his voice back down into normal range. "It was bad enough that they recognized me. Surely they have to assume there's at least a chance I was at that meet on official business. But then you basically just... tell them outright? The op is blown for sure, now."

"What op?" René said. "There was never any chance of anyone spilling their big secret to a fresh fish like you."

"If you thought that, why didn't you say so at the meeting? Before we got into this mess."

"No point. It was the only lead we had, so why not let it play out? I could, after all, have been wrong." René grinned at Dex, but he wasn't ready to forgive his friend just yet.

"Trouble in paradise?"

"Miss Annabelle!" René stood as if to move in for a hug, then seemed to remember Annabelle's preferences, nodded politely, and sat again. He gestured to a free chair and Annabelle joined them.

"René let the cat out of the bag," Dex said.

"I spoke with Jamie," René said to Annabelle. "I've known them a long time, and I trust them. Asking what they knew seemed like the most expedient thing to do. Besides, I wasn't about to harbour suspicions about one of my team without actually speaking to them about it. That's not how I operate."

"Okay," Annabelle said. "So? What did they say?"

"At first, they were pretty pissed off that I could even think such a thing," René said. "But then their analytical mind took over. Jamie is a fine investigator. They saw how we could make such a connection."

"And?"

"And they said no." René took a sip of his drink as if that were the end of it.

"That's it?" Dex asked. "You let it go at that?"

René shot Dex a look. "It was a half hour conversation, but it boiled down to *no*. No, Jamie didn't know of anyone from BBB who's ever said or done anything to make them think they might be involved." He shrugged. "What else do you expect? Larsen was right about one thing — you can't prove a negative."

The three of them sat there in silence for a moment, interrupted only when a waiter came by offering to bring Dex and Annabelle's abandoned drinks over to this table. They looked at each other, then nodded.

"So, does this have any impact on my plans for this meet up?" Dex asked.

René shook his head. "Obviously, Jamie will do the arithmetic. They know you're a plant. But they also think that the work their group is doing is worthwhile and that... others might agree. I think they'll let it play out."

The drinks arrived and the silence went on. It was slightly more companionable now, though. Slightly.

Annabelle broke it. "When he hears about this, Larsen is going to shit."

THE NEXT TWO DAYS passed uneventfully, but Dex felt like he was gearing up for a fight the whole time. He had arranged to go to a concert in M City with his old friend Maks, but he begged off at the last minute. He made an excuse about work, but really he couldn't stop thinking about what was going to happen with BBB. He was on edge and distracted and if something didn't give soon he didn't know what he was going to do.

When his system finally pinged with a message about the delivery, he nearly wept with the relief of it. Annabelle found him flopped out on the bed in the middle of the morning, working on some deep breathing exercises.

"You okay?"

"Mmmnf," Dex mumbled, then let his eyes slowly open. "I've been sleeping like shit, and every time my system has gone off I've had an adrenaline spike. I am worn the fuck out."

"I know you don't like them," Annabelle said softly, "but there are things to deal with that."

Stims. Yeah, Dex knew. He'd even looked into what might be the right mix, but then the BBB people had pinged. He could tell already that now the waiting was over, he'd be fine.

"I'm good," he said, sitting up. "The delivery's on. This afternoon."

"Oh!" She looked surprised. "I'd kind of assumed that it had been cancelled. You know—" She made a vague gesture that encompassed everything that had transpired in the last few days.

"Me, too," Dex said. "I guess René was right."

"Hope so," Annabelle said, her voice light but Dex knew there was a seed of real concern there.

"You want to come with me," he joked, "be my bodyguard?"

"Funny guy." She wasn't even smiling.

"Sorry." Dex stood and stretched, chagrin competing with stress as the dominant sensation in his body. "Like I said, I'll be glad when this is over."

"Well, there's some good news. Or, well, news anyway."

"Yeah?"

"We've done an analysis of all the Europa storefront attacks that fit the pattern. We think we've figured out when the next ones are likely to happen in Nice."

"That is good news. I was sure there was a pattern, but I couldn't figure it out well enough to make a prediction."

Annabelle nodded. "Apparently it's there. The computer analysis came up with an answer — I haven't had time to dig into it, it looks quite complex. But I guess we'll see if it's right. The analysis says it should be tomorrow night."

"That's... awfully specific."

"It gets better," Annabelle said. "Analysis thinks it's going to be an Empyre business in Riquier."

Dex blinked slowly. "There's a very finite number of potential targets," he said to Annabelle's growing smile. "Like, finite enough that we could theoretically have them all under surveillance." Her smile became a grin. "Well, I sure hope your computer knows what it's doing."

"We'll find out. Now, better go get ready to do your community service."

"Seems kind of pointless now," Dex said.

"Like you said, worst case scenario: you deliver some stuff to folks who need it. Not the most terrible way to spend an afternoon."

DEX KEPT ANNABELLE'S words in mind as he walked to the meeting point. The message had said to expect User923-N, the leader, but he didn't know who else would be there — he didn't know if *Jamie* would be there. He wasn't sure what to say to them if they were. Dex didn't like the feeling of being caught out as a spy.

Surely Jamie had told the rest of the group about him. He still didn't really understand why they had contacted him after all. Regardless of what he'd said to Annabelle, he couldn't shake the feeling that he was walking into a trap. But to what end?

He turned the corner and saw a familiar tall woman at the designated spot — User923-N. He scanned the area, but didn't recognize anyone else. That didn't mean she didn't have backup hidden nearby, but Dex felt a surge of confidence nonetheless. He strode toward her, trying to look natural. As natural as a modern urbanite could look given his implants and interfaces.

She caught his eye as he approached and subtly nodded, then turned to enter a warehouse-style building. He paused for a second, then followed her in.

The interior space wasn't large, but was stuffed with well-organized groupings of material. There were soft packages filled with what Dex guessed were clothes, boxes of food bricks and nutri-water, individual sanitation units in carry packs, some of the chiller/zapper units Dex had seen in the beach community. In the middle of the space were two of those large maglev hovering hand trucks.

"Glad you could make it, 428-C. We've found a new group of people living in Mont Boron. We'll be passing this stuff out — one of these per person," she gestured at the clothing bundles, "one each of the rest per shelter. This community is mainly couples and a few small groups and a few more singles. So I've figured three to one clothes to the other stuff. Got it?"

Dex nodded and began loading up one of the hand trucks. "How many units total?" he asked, nestling a sanitation unit on to the flat bed.

"Ten, maybe more," she said. "Let's go for an even dozen."

Dex grunted assent and kept humping goods. 923 was filling the other hand truck with great efficiency. He wondered how many of these deliveries she'd made.

When they had loaded the trolleys, 923 sent Dex a map file he could overlay on his visual system. It showed a circuitous route from their location to a point among the trees of Parc du Mont Boron. "This will take a few more minutes, but it will keep us away from the main street congestion."

"Concerned about being seen?" Dex asked, then wondered if he'd blown it by asking the question. 923 didn't seem fazed, though, and shook her head.

"No one cares about a couple of drones pushing cargo," she said. "We've just found that it actually is faster to take the longer, quieter route."

"Okay," Dex said. "Ready?"—

She nodded and led the way out of the warehouse. Dex wondered if it was some kind of test, to see if he'd abscond with the goods or abandon them. He followed, though, and in less than half an hour they had arrived at a surprisingly robust community hidden among the trees in the city's largest green space.

Dex worked his way through the group, distributing the goods as efficiently as possible. He found it hard not to stop and talk to the people there — all of them reminded him of himself, had his life taken one turn to the right rather than the left. Most of them were victims of layoff or firings, a couple were ideologically opposed to corporate work and there were a handful of artists, writers and musicians. When Dex encountered someone who fit that last group, he couldn't help himself and tried to talk them into finding an outlet in M City.

"It's not easy," he said to one woman, a painter, "but you can make real euros."

"But I don't do digital work," she said, pointing at the small colourful canvasses leaning against the board walls.

"Doesn't matter," Dex said. "I mean, digital is easier to

sell, sure, but there are people who want physical goods too. You can upload images or vid of the real item. And who knows, there might be people willing to pay for digital versions. You kind have to think about ways to expand what you do into other markets, but there are opportunities. And every little bit helps."

She frowned. "I don't really want this to become the same as working a job," she said, gesturing at her paintings. "This is meaningful for me. I don't want it to become a commodity."

Dex nodded. "I get it," he said. "I'm not trying to tell you what to do. But let me send you some links. Then at least you have something to base your decision on."

She looked unsure, but agreed. Dex sent her the files, then hurried to the next shelter.

When they were done, Dex and 923-N took the hand trucks back to the warehouse. They dropped them off, and 923 locked up the building.

"So," she said, "do you really think we would have anything to do with an operation that ends up in ordinary people getting fired and ending up on the street?"

Dex flushed, even thought it was an entirely legitimate question. "I have to pursue the leads I find," he said.

She nodded. "Well, I hope you realize that this one was a dead end." She tilted her head to one side, a shadow of a smile on her face. "Thank you for your help today, Andersson Dexter. If you're interested, we'd be happy to have you volunteer with us again."

She left without waiting for a response, which was for the best. Dex didn't have one.

TWENTY-THREE

DEX HAD TAKEN UP HIS POSITION in the back room of a JoocyMart, one of the Empyre businesses in Riquier, nearly three hours previously and his back was feeling every second of it. He was crammed into a break room space that was technically big enough for one person to sit and eat a meal, but breaks at Joocy were only ten minutes long. The room had clearly been designed partly to discourage sneaking extra down time.

He shifted his weight to try and work the pins and needles out of his legs, wondering what would happen if this store was the target. He would almost certainly fall on his face if he tried to jump on an intruder in his current state. He stood and began to sort of jiggle in place, trying to stay silent.

Waiting. It was the worst.

He sent in his periodic update to the local squad's board. René had called in his entire squad for the mission, but there weren't enough bodies to cover all the locations, so Dex volunteered. He'd been surprised when Biagini sent an official temporary deployment request to Mack Larsen. He'd been less surprised when Larsen approved it immediately. Annabelle had been deployed as well and was coordinating the online connections and public surveillance of the area. She'd even offered to take a shift at one of the businesses, but René managed to scrounge up enough other people so she could stick with her specialty.

To Dex, he'd admitted that it wasn't for Annabelle's comfort that he'd found another job for her.

"I'm afraid she might kill someone by mistake," he said, in all seriousness. Dex had seen her act from instinct a few times, once in an extreme situation. He knew that René's concerns weren't unfounded and she'd had a long, hard recovery from that one incident. It was better for them all that she stayed online.

"I have movement on Ribotti," Annabelle's calm, clear voice sounded in Dex's ear, as it would to all the other secreted members of the squad. "Two figures, wearing anti-recognition facepaint. Southbound from Barber."

That put them en route to Dex's location. He tensed, ready for a confrontation, then pulled up the map again. There were also four other potential targets which the possible assailants could be aiming for — he hadn't realized how many of the shops in this neighbourhood were subsidiaries of one firm.

He turned his system volume down to its lowest level, straining to hear any sound that could be coming from the street. Annabelle gave an update, putting the marks nearly on top of Dex's position. Time slowed. He forced his breathing to slow, feeling his body respond to the surge of adrenaline that naturally came with anticipation. He idly speculated about how many members of the squad were controlling their responses with stims. As he heard his pulse pound in his ears, he wondered how much it would have helped.

After what felt like a lifetime, Annabelle's voice told him

that they'd passed by the door to the JoocyMart, continuing south. An intense feeing of relief nearly buckled his knees, even as he knew that this didn't necessarily mean that he was in the clear. He had to remain vigilant — the people Annabelle were tracking could have been making a reconnaissance pass; they might not even be the attackers. Facepaint wasn't entirely uncommon, and while this was a fairly quiet area at this time of night, nowhere in the city was completely devoid of street activity at any time.

Dex fought to remain focussed but he still literally jumped when his system exploded in chatter. The two suspects had been apprehended after a brief altercation in a branch of the clothing store Mode.

They'd actually caught the storefront attackers.

DEX WASN'T PRESENT WHEN René and a couple of members of his team questioned the two people they had caught. He had gone home when the all clear was given, and when he got there found Annabelle finished with her part in the operation. With the people in custody in a safe house maintained by the squad, there was nothing left to do. They were both way too keyed up to just call it a night, though.

"What do you think is going to happen to Jamie if it turns out that the BBB people are involved?" Dex asked, idly.

"I guess that depends on whether there's any evidence that they knew but didn't do anything." Annabelle finished the glass of wine she'd poured before Dex had even made it back to the apartment. "Seems too soon to speculate on that."

"I know, I know." Dex paced the floor of the apartment. "I don't know what else to think about."

"We're not going to learn anything more tonight," Annabelle said. "We need to try and get some rest."

Dex nodded. "You're right. If there was ever a time for chemical assistance, this is probably it." He grabbed the small bottle of a sleeping tonic that he always kept handy, though somehow never used. "Six hour shot ought to do the job."

Annabelle nodded and took the measure Dex poured. She watched while he poured his own draught and they clicked their small glasses. "Here's to good news in the morning."

"I'll drink to that."

"YOU JUST LET THEM GO?"

Dex fought to keep the anger out of his voice. He knew it wasn't René's fault, that he'd had to release the suspects to the custody of the security department's team when they'd turned up. Long ago the organization had determined that they were adjacent to rather than in opposition to the security teams from the big firms. If their operations overlapped, handing things off to the corporate squad was the standard operating procedure. But Dex still couldn't really believe that René had just let the suspects walk away.

"We had them dead to rights," Dex carried on. "At least tell me that the security goons looked like they were going to finally do something about this. And how come they finally bothered to turn up at all? This is the first time Empyre sent out a team since these attacks began. Now that we did all the work, they're just going to swoop in and get the glory? No wonder someone is after them, if this is the way they operate."

After a short pause, René asked, "You done?"

"I guess," Dex answered, somewhat deflated but still upset.

"It wasn't a team from Empyre," René said but Dex didn't follow. His blank look prompted René to explain. "It was a Techloid security team that came for the people we caught."

The gears started working again in Dex's brain. "But Mode is an Empyre store, isn't it? We were only stationed in Empyre businesses, weren't we?" René nodded. "I'm lost. Why did Techloid show up and take custody of our suspects?"

"Because they were Techloid employees." René said and let that sink in.

"What?!"

"I did not get a strong impression that security was there to reprimand the individuals, either. I am quite certain that our quarry got a message out to the Techloid goons who came to rescue their people."

Dex's jaw was literally hanging open as he put it all together. Part of him was in total surprise but a smaller part of him felt like he should have seen this all along. They'd all been so sure that this was some kind of misplaced grassroots activism that they'd completely ignored the other possibilities.

"Inter-corporate sabotage," he finally said. "That's what this has been all along. Empyre and Techloid, waging a petty little war against each other." He shook his head. "How could I have missed this?"

René shrugged. "It's easy to see it now, but this is not how the firms have done business in my lifetime at least. There's no reason we should have thought they'd changed their tactics so dramatically."

Dex shook his head. "The signs were all there. All those incursions into each others' territories. The spying, undermining each others' operations. This was just another volley in that same battle."

"So it would appear."

"Well, what are we going do now?"

René pursed his lips. "Something tells me that getting caught isn't going to be enough to stop this operation. I imagine they might change their schedule, maybe even mix up the targets, but if Empyre and Techloid are bound and determined to try and put each other out of business, nothing we do is going to stop them."

Dex thought for a moment. "Maybe nothing we do can stop them, but it's not just us anymore."

René cocked an eyebrow.

"Maybe something useful did come out of me chasing the wrong lead all this time," Dex said.

IT WOULD PROBABLY BE the last time they'd all meet in the M City squad boardroom like this. Larsen had made no bones about the fact that he resented the time they'd all wasted on the storefront attacks.

"It's not our job to police the firms," he repeated, standing at the head of the table while the rest of the assembled group sat. "Even if we wanted to, we can't. I'm sure none of us like that fact, but it is a fact. We exist to take up the slack where the firms don't operate. That's it — and that's plenty." He glared at each individual avatar around the table.

Captain Zhang pushed her chair away from the table and stood slowly. "Mack, I take your point, I really do, but it's not entirely accurate."

Larsen looked like he was about to defend his position,

but Zhang put up a hand to silence him. And it actually worked.

"What we did in here," she went on, gesturing expansively, "was in direct opposition to action that was being taken by some of the firms to try and restrict activity online. Whether it was purposely to make life more difficult for freelancers or just to solidify their own positions didn't matter — it didn't matter to the people they were hurting and it didn't matter to those of us who fought against it. All of us in this room," she looked directly at Mack Larsen, "all of us made a decision then that we had to oppose that action by the firms. This is no different. In the virtual world or in the physical world, we have to do what we can to even out the opportunities for ordinary people. That's our mandate, and it always has been. Justice, or at least as much justice as we can offer, for people who don't have access to it any other way."

Larsen's expression didn't change, but he sat back down and kept quiet. René cleared his throat and gave Captain Zhang a quick look. She smiled and sat, then René went on as if the entire previous conversation hadn't occurred.

"Dex has made a tenuous but, we think, viable connection with the Nice group that organized through *Better Biz Brigade*. They are already working on the streets to do what they can to help people who are on the margins and we already have someone else as an active part of the group."

"Jamie Eristo," Susana Bells said. "What is their status at the moment?"

"Still an active member of my squad," René said. "Probably not as thrilled with some of us as they once were, but I think they'll be on board. After some apologies are made." René shot Dex a sympathetic look.

"These people are doing good work," Dex said. "They're

putting themselves on the line to help people and they have resources. I don't know where their supplies come from, but they have connections, skills, and offer real solutions."

"So," Larsen said, "you're saying they have the means, motive and opportunity to actually help make a change?"

Someone snickered, but Dex just nodded. "Yes, sir. And I aim to work with them, whether it's official or not. I happen to think we can do a lot more good if it is official, but..." He let the thought trail off, knowing that he'd made his point.

Eventually Larsen nodded once, which was the closest they were going to come to him admitting that he'd been wrong. That was fine. Now they just had to figure out what they could actually do to make a difference.

TWENTY-FOUR

"WELL, THAT COULD HAVE BEEN WORSE." Dex tore open the pack of cigarettes and lit one, pulling deeply on the simulated smoke. His implants gave him the sensation of *something* filling his lungs, a slight tingling sensation as he held the smoke in, and the calming experience of slowly exhaling. He almost understood why people once poisoned themselves for this experience.

"Mmm," Annabelle agreed, a large drink materializing before her. "I'm starting to see why you dislike Larsen so much."

"It's not really his fault. He's spent his whole career trying to make people realize that it's just as important to protect all this," he twirled a finger in the air, "as it is to help people out there. No wonder he's a bit reluctant to look outward again."

Annabelle nodded. "You know I'm on his side of that argument," she said, "but until we develop some way to lose the meat sacks, we're all stuck with needing food and shelter out there. It wouldn't matter if we could turn M City into a free paradise, that would still be true." She took a long sip of her drink, a look of pleasure crossing her face at the sensation. "And when *I'm* arguing for physicality, you know it must be serious."

Dex laughed. "True enough." He swirled the dark liquid in his faceted highball glass and toasted her. "So, what now?"

"Now, I'm going to help BBB close that security hole in their user database."

Dex made a face. "They'll probably figure out what we did."

She nodded. "You aren't the only one with some apologies to make. I knew it might come back to bite me when I did it, and I'm willing to take responsibility. Hopefully they'll accept a pro-bono fix as at least a partial atonement. If not, well, I guess my name will get dragged through the digital mud. My freelancing days might well be over before they really even got started." She shrugged, like it was no big deal, but Dex could tell that this was hard for her.

"I'm sure there's a way to see you out of it—"

"No. If we're going to be working with these people, it has to be with all that suspicion and secrecy behind us. Whatever happens to me, I can handle it."

"I know," Dex said. "I just wish things had gone differently."

"Mistakes happen. We can't avoid that. I'll be fine."

Dex reached out for her hand and squeezed. He hoped that she was right.

DEX WASN'T LOOKING FORWARD to seeing Jamie Eristo again. He didn't think they'd be likely to ever regain the camaraderie they'd once had, but that wasn't the issue. Dex was certain that Jamie would be professional at a minimum. The problem was that Dex knew he'd suspected Jamie of being involved in the attacks. He hasn't really believed it, but he'd been open to the possibility. And now, knowing that's what he'd thought, it was hard to look Jamie in the eye.

But, uncomfortable as it was, it had to be done. Dex was the link between BBB and the rest of the organization. He was, as he'd often been before, the bridge between the virtual and physical worlds. In another circumstance, he might have found the irony amusing, though it probably was his scepticism of the idea that embracing virtuality was all it took to liberate people from the vicissitudes of the mundane that let him walk both worlds so easily. Or maybe he was just full of shit and getting lost in his own thoughts was a way to distract him from the meeting he was on his way to.

Dex had been surprised when User923-N suggested Dex meet the rest of the group at the warehouse. He'd have assumed they changed locations frequently — or at least would have abandoned that spot since he had been there. They must not be as suspicious as he was, a thought that made a fresh wave of guilt crash over him.

He slid open the door, senses on high alert. The warehouse was now bare, even the hand trucks were gone. Maybe the group wasn't as trusting as he'd thought. They were all there waiting for him, the same five people he'd met at the park. They faced him in a line and Dex had a brief flash of an interrogation. This would be a fine location for such a thing. He was thankful that he'd had the forethought to let Annabelle know exactly where he was going.

He closed the door behind himself and walked toward the group, the sound of his footsteps echoing off the high ceiling. He couldn't read the expression on Jamie's face and decided that there was no point in trying to anticipate how this was going to go down. He'd find out soon enough anyway.

"Nice to see you again," the leader said with a cool smile. "I understand that our group is no longer under suspicion of being involved in the attacks on local businesses over the past few months?"

"That's correct," Dex said, keeping it simple.

She nodded and no one else spoke. Dex focussed on breathing slowly and evenly, ready to run if he had to. He didn't want to fight — he hoped it wouldn't come to that. He wished he hadn't closed the warehouse door.

Finally, she turned to the two people on either side of her and they moved to a darkened area behind her. They came back with a pallet of folding chairs and began to set them up.

"I don't hold your suspicions against you," she said, then glanced toward Jamie. "None of us do. Oh, don't get me wrong, being on the inside, it was hard to understand why anyone would think we could be involved, but the idea that resistance must be violent — it's an old, entrenched idea. Even among like-minded people," she gestured to include Dex in the group, "it's easy to think that there are people who just want to fuck things up. Who don't see the collateral damage or don't care. I believe those people exist. So I can't be too upset when someone else might see me that way."

"I'm glad to hear you say that," Dex said, "and for whatever it's worth, I am sorry I got it so wrong." He turned to face Jamie. "I thought I had a lead and I wasn't willing to let it go, no matter where it took me. I'm not sorry for that, but I am sorry I didn't trust you."

Jamie's mouth opened, but before they could say anything, they caught the leader's eye and simply nodded. Dex had a feeling that he'd gotten off easy because of that look.

"I'd like to move forward if we can," the leader said. "Your organization has resources that we do not and vice versa. Together we could be greater than the sum of our parts and I'd like to see what we could accomplish."

"As would I," Dex said. "Let's see what we can do to make that happen."

DEX SPENT THE NEXT several hours with the group brainstorming ideas. They agreed that the first step would be to publicize as much as they knew about the battle between Empyre and Techloid. Given that the perpetrators were in the wind, their evidence was circumstantial, but it was still compelling. People ought to know that the firms were sabotaging each other and regular employees were being caught in the crossfire. Dex offered to set the plan in motion and was feeling like things had gone as well as he could have hoped as he walked back to the apartment.

He passed through Place du Général de Gaulle on his way and was struck with a sudden understanding. The pieces were all coming together and it was almost like a ten gig download hitting his head: hard and heavy, individual packets coalescing into readable data. The sabotage on Electrois which led to the explosion... Electrois and Techloid were both owned by Vertisales... Was Empyre targeting more than just Techloid shops? Where they going after all of Vertisales?

It was too much of a coincidence to be anything else. There was no proof, but the sabotage on Electrois had been systematic and subtle. Exactly the kind of work that Annabelle had been asked to do by Omnitrack, exactly the kind of work that Dex imagined a corporate black ops team would do. He wondered if they'd even have suspected BBB if Empyre had left the shops alone.

He walked the rest of the way back to the apartment in a daze. If only he could prove that this was part of Empyre's plan, it would surely galvanize people into opposing them. Several people had been hurt. Lennox Sessa died. Even if people could ignore the effects of the storefront attacks, they couldn't ignore this.

But without someone on the inside, Dex couldn't see how they could prove that Empyre was responsible. And getting an insider to spill seemed like an impossible task. Maybe the speculation would be enough. Maybe just presenting the evidence they did have and letting people draw their own conclusions would lead them to the same place as it had Dex. They had to try.

ANNABELLE WAS WORKING WHEN Dex arrived home, but she messaged him that she'd be done soon. He organized some food while he waited for her to finish up, pondering their next move. He was so deep in thought that Annabelle's voice startled him.

"How did it go? Was Jamie okay with you?"

"It was fine," Dex said. "Actually, I don't see how it could have gone better. I think Jamie's pissed at me personally, but they're a professional. I think deep down they know that if the roles had been reversed, they'd have done the same thing. I'm sure that doesn't stop them feeling a bit betrayed, but I don't think we'll have a problem working together. In either organization."

"So, they've accepted you — us, I suppose — as part of the group?"

Dex nodded and held out a food brick to Annabelle. She

shook her head, so he tore off the wrapper to take a bite.

"We worked out a plan to share what we know the firms have been doing. It's time that more than just a few of us knew what was happening behind the scenes."

"I'm glad your meeting worked out." She sounded genuinely pleased, but Dex detected a note of something else in her voice.

"How about you?" he asked.

"My contacts at BBB were somewhat less willing to forgive and forget," she said.

"Oh, no."

She shrugged. "It's not catastrophic. They accepted my help to close the security hole I climbed through to jimmy with your account. But they've made it clear that they don't want to work with me — or anyone who recommended me — in the future."

"Ouch," Dex said. "I'm guessing that Stella Bish isn't going to be your best friend when she gets wind of that."

Annabelle shook her head. "I've already been cut loose."

"Oh, Annabelle, I'm so sorry." Dex took her hand but she pulled it away, an apologetic look on her face.

"Bish was quite decent about it. Somehow she knew what had gone down with the investigation and she said she was sympathetic, but business was business and she had to distance herself from me for a while. She said that she'd be in touch later, but..." She made a face. "Who knows when that will be."

"So, what are you going do?"

"Look for work on my own, I guess. Bish handles a lot of clients but not everyone. I've got a small job on the line already. Plus, I can try to get more shifts with Larsen, maybe moonlight for some of the other squads. I'll manage. But it's going to be tight for a while."

"We'll make it work," Dex said, forcing himself to keep from going to her. He knew she needed her own space now, but it was so hard. If he were the one hurting, he'd want her to hold him. But it wasn't him.

"I never should have left Omnitrack," she said in a small voice.

"Don't say that. Especially now. What they were doing was wrong; do you really think that you could have stayed there when they were asking you to basically do what we've discovered Empyre was doing?" He explained what he'd figured out about the Electrois explosion. "And sabotaging a train network — the ways that could go wrong, I just don't even want to think about it."

"You're right," Annabelle said, "but it's so hard when there aren't a lot of other options. And even now I'm so much luckier than most people — I have skills and connections, I have you. I can make it work without a regular job. What about everyone else who doesn't have that? How are they supposed to say no when their bosses come asking for them to do something like this?"

Dex didn't say anything. What could he say when he didn't have an answer?

TWENTY-FIVE

"I'M GLAD I COULD USE MY FREE SPACE FOR THIS," Zahara Zhang said to Dex as she gave him the nickel tour of the kiosk she and some members of her squad had set up in M City. They'd put up the footage from the takedown at Mode, along with an explanation of the evidence they'd collected showing that the storefront attacks appeared to be carried out by the same people. They even had actual vid of the Techloid security team collecting their people, admitting that they were Techloid employees. It was a good set up.

"This is a great way to make this information public," Dex said. "It's safe here and easily accessible. How hard was it to organize?"

"No problem at all," Zhang said. "The visual interface for rezzing the block is really easy to use. Whoever thought up that maintenance room idea was a genius."

Dex remembered their earlier visit and the broken holo message. "You find any other little notes from your benefactor?"

"No," Zhang laughed, then got a strange look on her face. "Though I did have to use the full admin panel for one thing, and I thought I saw something odd..." A schematic panel appeared on a wall next to her. "Hang on. I want to check something out."

She minimized the schematic with a pinch of her fingers, then an old-fashioned text screen appeared in its place.

"Not the command line," Dex groaned.

"Exactly the command line," Zhang said, a string of characters appearing on the screen. The screen was a now a cacophony of text, some that was comprehensible enough to Dex — filenames, search results — but much of it was the gobbledygook that gave him a headache.

```
$ cd /
$ ls
net             bin             opt
network         cores           private
system          dev             sbin
etc             hello.holo      tmp
home            usr             var
hello.dict      setup.log       setup.pkg
```

"I think there might be a text version of that holo," Zhang said. "It's worth a shot."

```
$ more hello.dict

Hello Zahara Zhang,

If your seeing this I must be dead sorry but I always
wanted to say that. Not that I'm happy to be dead,
but, well, nevermind. I have or I suppose I should
say had a flair for the dramatic.

Anyway you're probably wondering who I am, why I let
the disk block to you. As for the former, no one
important. Which is how I manage this all along.

As for why you? Well. Why not you. I thought you'd
use it well.

You see we met once as part of your initiative to
```

```
help secure the MCity interface. I distributed some
upgrade rods for you. I was using another name I
don't expect you remember me.

As you may have guessed, this disk block is one of
many. Not enough for a big firm to mess, but enough
to add a significant number to the private supply.
It's not enough but it's start.

Mr. clock is yours to do with as you see fit. Make a
living for yourself, give the space away to a
collective or sell it back to some firm. I don't
care. Just do with that what you think is right. It's
about time that individual people were making those
decisions.
```

"Well, that was certainly interesting," Zhang said, "if not exactly illuminating."

"What's with all the weird stuff? *Mister clock?*" Dex asked.

"Speech-to-text error, I think." Zhang said. "Automated from the voice message that was part of the holo."

"Oh, yeah. That makes sense." Dex said. "Well, I guess we have learned one thing from this."

"What's that?"

"Irina Nightingale would probably be pleased with what we're doing with this rez space."

Zhang smiled. "You're right. She probably would."

IT'S NOT LIKE DEX thought they were going set the world on fire. He never even really expected anything concrete to come of it immediately. He was a realist, he thought. He did, however, expect people to care.

The public reaction to the revelation that two of the major firms were actively working to sabotage each other was, to put it mildly, disappointing. The day they released the evidence it was a trending topic in some of the feeds. The online chatter seemed to indicate that no one seriously doubted the evidence; the problem was that the most people regarded it as a matter of idle curiosity.

And of course, there were the few, vocal critics. Some argued that it was business as usual, others that the evidence was fabricated. The analysis was that these claims were essentially dismissed but it didn't change the fact that, all in all, the news made as much of a splash as a raindrop in the ocean.

Dex wanted to mope around, annoyed at the little effect they'd had, but he forced himself to get on with his work. Annabelle had every right to mope around — she'd been hustling to find more freelance work, and had done a couple of small jobs since being let go by Stella Bish, but they were nothing compared to the work she was used to. And they didn't bring in a lot, either. Mack Larsen had thrown as much work her way as he could, but most of the organization's activities weren't exactly lucrative. The whole point of their existence was that they helped people regardless of their financial value.

But even though by all rights she ought to be upset about her situation, Annabelle seemed to be making the best of it. So much so that she was the one who forced Dex to keep up with his social commitments.

"How can I go off and just have fun at a time like this?" he'd said when she reminded him that he'd agreed to get back to rehearsing with his band.

"A time like what?"

"This! Everything has turned to shit and no one seems to care. There are more people out on the streets every day. Empire and Techloid and Omnitrack and fuck knows who else are taking aim at each other with no concern for the consequences to anything but their own gross holdings statements. And here..." He broke off, wishing he hadn't bought up their own personal situation.

"Yes," Annabelle prompted. "What about here?"

Dex sighed. "You're working so hard to get things going again. For work. For this." He spread his arms out, taking in the apartment and everything in it. Neither of them having corporate jobs meant that they had to pay for it all out of pocket, which they were now only barely managing. "How can I just fuck off to some M City dive bar to bang on my mandolin while you're out there hustling for another couple of euros?"

"Oh, honey," Annabelle smiled sadly. "Yeah, I'm trying to get things back off the ground, and yeah, it's a lot of work. But even I take an hour or two off here and there. I know we've gotten ourselves..." she looked around the apartment, "entangled here. And that's mostly a good thing. But I'm capable of taking care of myself. And if you really believe that giving up everything in life that you love is taking care of yourself," she shot him a look. "Then maybe you're not so much more than a pretty face after all."

"Everything I love is right here," Dex answered after a moment.

Annabelle shook her head. "You are a sweet-talker, there was never any doubt of that, but we both know that's not true. You need your music nights, your drinks with René down at Le Rétro, your puzzles to solve just as much as you need food bricks and water." Dex opened his mouth to argue, but she put her finger to his lips and silenced him.

"I know you'd give up all that for me. Whether I want you to or not, I get it. But the point is you don't have to. You're a much better partner to me when you're not miserable, and going to a rehearsal and playing a gig or two keeps you from being miserable."

Dex nodded but he wasn't won over. "What about everything else? There are people who barely have enough to eat while I'm off gallivanting...."

"You're right, it's not fair," she said, "and I don't really have a good answer for that, except that you being miserable doesn't make their lives any better. And as far as I can tell, you being less miserable doesn't make their lives any worse. I guess that's the thing — try to live the best life you can while making sure that it doesn't happen on someone else's back."

"But how can I be sure?"

They were both silent for a while. "I guess that's why we're doing what we're doing," she said, finally. "Trying to make things more transparent, so people know what's really going on behind the stuff we buy and the tools we use. It's so we can be sure."

ANNABELLE EVENTUALLY KICKED DEX out of the house, so he went to meet up with René at Le Rétro. He felt badly about spending money when things were so tight, but she'd insisted. He took the long way to get there, along the beach and though the Pietonne. He couldn't help but think about how lucky he was to live somewhere so beautiful, with work he liked and people he loved. How did the bosses at the firms survive, knowing they were the beneficiaries of so much unfairness? Could they honestly believe that an accident of birth entitled them to so much more than the vast majority of the world's population? Did they even recognize the people they employed to generate their profits as the same as them?

He stepped across the threshold of Le Rétro half an hour later and in a foul mood. René took one look at his expression and said, "You, sir, look like you could use an attitude adjuster." He jerked his head toward the bar.

Dex shook his head. "Just water for me," he said, rubbing his fingers together in the gesture he'd learned from René indicated that something was expensive.

"Hmm," René said. "Annabelle's work situation?"

Dex nodded.

"Well, I can spring for a rum once in a while," René said, poking the menu pad before Dex could protest. "It's in my own self interest to have you less owly."

"Owly?" Dex was thrown off balance by the bizarre turn of phrase.

"Look it up," René said, laughing. "It suits you today."

Dex did just that and had to admit that René was right. He *was* cranky.

"I'm just so tired, René." He took a deep breath and consciously willed his muscles to relax. "It's not like I'm overworked or anything — other than a couple of hours here and there to help out with some deliveries, nothing in my day to day has really even changed. But it's always there now. Thinking about how unfair things are, worrying if what I'm doing is making things better or helping this fucked up system carry on destroying people's lives."

The server brought their drinks and Dex lifted his glass. "Who made this?" he said. "How do I know that the company I'm supporting by buying this drink isn't part of Empyre or Vertisales?"

"Number one," René said, "you could look it up. Number two, technically you're not buying that drink."

"You know what I mean." René nodded. "And yeah, I

could look it up. I should, really. But even if it's no one we know about, there's no way to know how well they treat their employees. I mean, when you think about it no one really treats their employees *well*. The entire system is built on all of us being stuck — requiring a job just to get by, so we have no choice but to go along with what our bosses want."

"It's better than it was a few years ago," René said. "Look at us. Annabelle. Everyone in La Liberté. We've all gotten out of the system; it can be done."

"Sure. But how many of us are there? Is it even one percent?"

René frowned. "I don't know."

Dex took a sip of his drink, his mind spiralling down into the thoughts that he'd been keeping at bay until now. "And then I have to wonder, are we really making things better by getting out of the system?"

"What do you mean?" René asked. "Surely this is better."

"For *us* it is," Dex said, "but did you notice that it was only when people started freelancing, setting up shop in M City, that the firms tried to control the online space? Then when we took that back, and when places like La Liberté started up, that's when the firms got aggressive with each other. I guess that if they couldn't take us on to regain their lost market share, they had to turn on each other."

René's voice was quiet, but intense. "Are you trying to say that this is our fault?"

Dex shrugged unhappily. "Unintended consequences, maybe. Of course, none of us expected this to happen, maybe no one could have even predicted it. But I can't ignore the pattern, René."

"I know you dislike coincidences," René said, "but correlation isn't the same as causation."

"I know," Dex said. "But it's not just the timing. It's logical, in a horrible way."

René stared off into the distance, but Dex didn't think his old friend was online. He was working it out, pondering this terrible reality that had been building in Dex's mind over the past weeks. Finally, he lifted an eyebrow and looked at Dex.

"You might be right," he admitted. "It does all follow. But I don't know if it changes anything. First, we can't go back in time. We have to deal with the situation is it exists now, and fretting about how things might have gone differently won't change anything. Second," he took a deep breath. "Even knowing everything that happened, I'm not sure we should have done anything differently."

"Really?" Dex asked, genuinely confused. "There are people who have lost everything. At least one person has died as a part of all this. And you wouldn't change anything?"

"I said I don't know," René answered. "How many people have been helped by the changes we made — all those people working for themselves in M City, even out here? Where would they have been otherwise? Would they be on the streets or worse?" He shook his head. "I honestly don't know. Maybe we should have just let well enough alone, kept our heads down and not tried to change anything." He narrowed his eyes and leaned in, voice low. "That feels so wrong to me, but I don't know. Maybe it would have been better. But it's too late for would have beens. This is reality," he thumped the table with one hand. "We have to work with this, the way things are now. That's all we can do."

"You're right," Dex said, finally. "Of course. I just—" He closed his eyes, the deep truth of what had been bothering him finally coming to the surface. "I'm just terrified of making another mistake. Of making another decision that I think will make things better but it doesn't. Pushing the firms into making more decisions that hurt people. It seems like everything I do lately has some terrible consequence. Annabelle..." He didn't finish the thought.

"Ah." René said. "Miss Annabelle's work troubles because of the BBB operation."

Dex nodded miserably.

"Well, I cannot help with that," René said. "Of course, she would probably be more displeased that you think she is your responsibility than she is upset about this consequence."

"What?"

René gave a small chuckle. "You love her very much, we can all see that. But you are not her guardian, you are not her keeper. She makes her own decisions, as you well know, and she has no interest in being mollycoddled. Not everything is your responsibility, Dex. You are not the saviour of the universe, not even the saviour of your lady love. She is her own hero. As it should be."

TWENTY-SIX

DEX TOOK RENÉ'S WORDS TO HEART and, although he couldn't stop feeling guilty, he tried not to act on those feelings. He needed to figure out how to be supportive to Annabelle without telling her what to do. He should be spending time with the local BBB group actually helping rather than complaining. In both cases, he knew what to do, but it was sometimes hard to remember to do it. He was getting better, though, ever so slowly.

Annabelle had kept making him go to his band rehearsals and now they'd even lined up a gig in M City. Dex still felt weird about it, but if all went well he'd actually bring in a little money. At least, it wouldn't cost anything, so he didn't have that to feel guilty about.

Annabelle's work situation had improved slightly, though she was still locked out of the most lucrative contracts. Luckily, Stella Bish had a slightly overinflated opinion of her influence, and there were enough people and organizations who needed coding help and who weren't her exclusive clients. Annabelle was starting to develop contacts and references on her own. It was slow but it was steady.

Slow. That was the word that described everything. Dex

knew that the little they could do wasn't going to change anything overnight — he sometimes felt like it probably wouldn't change anything at all — but he couldn't help but feel frustrated.

The details about how Vertisales and Empyre were sabotaging each other's holdings were available for anyone to see at the kiosk in Captain Zhang's disk block. It still wasn't the biggest news of the day, but in some corners it had gotten people talking. Some people had begun adding anonymous reports, including a few that were similar to Annabelle's experience at Omnitrack. All in all, over a half dozen different umbrella companies were now implicated in predatory practices, representing hundreds of brands. It was nearly impossible to keep track.

On one hand, Dex was heartened to see that people were adding information to the pool. Knowing what these companies were up to was the first necessary step in fighting them. And of course, if ordinary people knew about it, the bosses at those companies' competitors would know. But could anything really be done to protect the people who worked there?

DEX WAS LOADING A transport cube with the components for sturdy prefabricated housing, which the BBB group was helping to construct in the Mont Boron park. The people he'd met previously had decided to make a permanent home there and enough of them had found ways of making a bit of cash that they had managed to buy some cut-rate shelter units from a wholesaler. They'd needed a delivery address and transportation, which BBB had been able to provide. Plus some willing grunt labour.

"This is the last one."

"Thanks, Kora," Dex said, taking the final crate from the leader of the group. She'd finally told him her name the previous week — trust came slowly to her, but Dex understood that. He carefully stowed the box in the transport, then sealed up the vehicle. He gave it a couple of loud smacks, and Mikkel, one of the other volunteers, set it on its programmed route to the building site.

Dex flopped onto a nearby chair and wiped his face with the hem of his shirt. "This feels like we're really making a difference," he said. "Even if we're just acting as glorified couriers. I'm impressed that they managed to scrape together enough money to get these so quickly. It must have been some bargain they found."

Kora smiled enigmatically, then appeared to come to a decision.

"There are bargains... and bargains," she said, emphasizing the words with her hands.

"Are you telling me these housing units fell off the back of a truck?"

She laughed. "Not in the way you mean. They aren't stolen. Exactly."

"What does that mean?"

She looked at him, pondering. "You used to have a corporate job, right?" Dex nodded. "Ever in management?"

He laughed, a short, sharp sound. "You're kidding, right?"

She shook her head. "It isn't that much different in the management suites than it is in the bullpens. Sure, there are perks — I'm not denying that. But you've still got your quotas, your ridiculous requirements, your daily terror of being demoted. There are plenty of people wearing management uniforms who aren't happy with the system. A few of them are even in places like the Brigade."

She gave Dex a significant look and he was pretty sure he understood what she was telling him. Aside from himself and Jamie, Dex had no idea what the rest of the group did for work. He'd assumed most of them were freelancers but figured that some of them were still working low level corp jobs. It had never occurred to him that they might be higher up, but Kora was right. Why not? And more specifically, why not her?

"Okay, sure. But what exactly does that have to do with scoring a sweet bargain?"

Kora leaned back in her chair, and crossed one long leg over the other. "Being in management is strange. You're kind of stuck between two worlds. On one hand, you're the representative of the employer to all the people below you. You appear to have power, but you don't, not really. Almost all your decisions are dictated either directly from a superior, or more usually, though the procedures. There's not that much room to maneuver with respect to the people. But on the other hand, you often have a lot of control over the goods. Pulse pricing, stock liquidation, consolidation... some management positions basically handle all that without a significant amount of oversight. There are lots of ways to move things around that are in complete accordance with the procedures and head office strategies, but that can have... additional benefits."

Dex took a moment to make sense of what she was saying.

"So, you — or someone — can basically decide that a bunch of housing units need to be sold off on the cheap and then you..."

"Or *someone*," Kora said, smirking.

"Someone can sell them to a group that might not be able to afford them otherwise."

Kora nodded. "That kind of thing is possible, yes."

Dex frowned, another thought coming into his head. "Could you — I mean, someone — do that with entire sub-brands?"

Kora cocked her head. "I... don't know about that specifically. Maybe? Can you give me an example?"

"Yeah, I think I can."

Keeping the details out of it, Dex described what he knew about Irina Nightingale, Colex and Oyuba.

"So," Kora said, "you're thinking that over a couple of years some manger consolidated a bunch of subsidiaries from their firm into a single sub-brand, which was then liquidated... to their own private ownership?"

Dex nodded.

"I can't see why not," she said. "Liquidation is common enough. Firms change market focus and their existing holdings become liabilities. If the manager could afford the price that head office wants to get, sure. They could buy up a bunch of product, why not?"

"And then they could turn around and give it all away?"

"What?"

"Uh, I mean if they wanted to, you know, theoretically?"

"Well, you can do whatever you want with your own goods," Kora said. "Once they own it, they can be Robin Hood if they want to." She thought for a moment. "You know, that's not a bad idea. A great way to use the firm's own policies against itself, all totally within the bounds of your contractual obligation." A smile grew on her face. "I think I like this theoretical person of yours."

WHEN HE GOT BACK to the apartment, Dex linked into his M City office. His conversation with Kora had given him an idea. *Better Biz Brigade* seemed to be a clearinghouse for people who were trying to change the system, which was what it looked more and more likely that Irina Nightingale was trying to do with her bequests. Dex wondered if it wasn't an entirely unique strategy.

He logged into the BBB boards, his user ID now at a trusted level through legitimate usage. There was a robust integrated search and Dex spent a few minutes refining his parameters.

He fought off disappointment when his search only brought up two posts that referenced leaving gifts in a will, but all that changed when he read the second post. It was made by Irina Nightingale, he was sure of it. The details were obscure, and the posts' author was listed only as BBB's typically anonymous User235-K, but Dex found it impossible to believe that the exact process he'd determined that Nightingale used would be described by someone else, down to the number of disk blocks she'd ended up controlling.

There was nothing in the post that was news to Dex, but now he had a user ID. He called up the list of all posts made under that ID, then had his system scan for relevant keywords. While the script worked, he grabbed a food brick from the box. Annabelle was online, but must have seen him through her overlay.

"How was your shift with BBB?"

"I'm sore all over," Dex said, "but the conversation was enlightening."

"Oh?"

He told Annabelle about what Kora had said, and as he spoke, she blinked a couple of times as she fully focussed on the apartment.

"So she thinks that there are people in management who are sympathetic? And you think that Irina Nightingale was one of them?"

Dex nodded.

"I wonder how many of them there are," Annabelle said, "and how we could reach them? We could use people on the inside."

"I think we probably already are reaching them," Dex said, explaining about finding Nightingale's posts on BBB. "It's just a matter of slowly making changes."

Annabelle made a face. "It's all too slow for me," she said. "And way too slow for Lennox Sessa."

"I know," Dex said, dropping his hand to her shoulder and resting it there for the briefest moment before pulling away again. "All the more reason we have to keep at it, even when it feels pointless."

Dex's system pinged then, indicating that his search was completed.

"Duty calls," he said with a small smile.

"No rest for the wicked," Annabelle responded but with little joy as she refocussed online.

Back in the office, Dex called up the results of his search. He skimmed them and found little of interest until he came to a long post by User235-K dated only a few weeks before Captain Zhang had received her inheritance.

> I was just a nameless, faceless middle manager, the same as a thousand others in the firm I worked for. But unlike them, I believed that we can do better. Not as a company, as a society.

I saw what people were doing online, in M City, creating small pockets of independence. And I saw how the firms were fighting back. It's a war, a cold one maybe, but there are battle lines being drawn. I could see it happening even inside the firm. Consolidation and expansion, anything to keep the market share being eroded. But the people who pay the cost are people like you and me — people who work for a living, people who need the goods and services we create.

I don't like it. I don't like the power that the firms have over everyone: management, employee, customer. And the only way to reduce their power is to redistribute it. So that's what I've done.

I chose my beneficiaries based on several criteria. Some were people who needed help, some were people who were on the forefront of making a change already. But they were all ordinary people who deserve an opportunity to finally help make the decisions that affect them.

I hope that the little I have done here will help the cause, in as much as there is such a thing. Maybe my small life won't have been entirely in vain. As I've learned, it's all we can hope for, in the end.

Twenty-Seven

DEX LINKED DIRECTLY INTO THE BACKSTAGE area of The Sidetrack, the bar where he and the rest of Chemical Celeste would be playing their first show in over a year. His avatar was dapper as always in his tailored pinstripe suit, but back in the closet office in Nice he was awash in nervous sweat. He was always a little nervous before he began to play for an audience, but this was worse than usual. Their rehearsals had been rocky to start, but he was sure they'd gotten their vibe back over the last few weeks. But it was one thing to play alone in a cheap rented shared space and another entirely to play to a bar full of paying punters.

The keyboardist and bandleader, Javier, had been at this longer than any of the rest of them. He'd been playing in bands long before he'd formed Chemical Celeste, and he gave them all a quick pep talk.

"It's always tough to get back into it after a break," he said, "but we're tight. We've been sounding great the last few rehearsals, so I know that we just have to let it flow. Besides, one of the great things about playing in here is that you can turn off whatever you want. You know that the audience response really takes the music to the next level, but if at first they're freaking you out, just make them disappear. Don't want to hear the applause — turn it off. You could even do it all by ear if you wanted to," he paused, "but you might miss a cue. On second thought, maybe don't turn off everything."

The rest of them laughed nervously, but Javier's calming voice had been enough to remind them of how much fun it could be to play for an audience. Dex remembered that he had more experience at this than any of the others except for Javier. He took a breath and picked up his cheap mandolin in Nice. He plucked a couple of strings, hearing the sound both in the confines of the small office and in his implants thought the M City interface. It was weird, but he was used to it by now.

On the other side of the stage door, the emcee was finishing her warmup set. "Let's go put on a show," Javier said, grinning at the rest of the band. He got a set of nervous grins in response, then they linked onto the stage in their arranged places — Arvind on the drums in the rear, Suzi, Dex, Kandace and Javier forming a line in front. Arvind called out a one, two, one, two, three, four, and Suzi blew the opening strains of their first number on her trumpet.

They started with a slow song they'd been playing since they first started playing together, a song they all knew forwards and backwards. From the first note Dex felt like he'd fallen into a well worn pattern, his fingers finding their places without thought. As they made their way through the set, the songs got more complex but they each rose to the occasion. All the practice paid off, along with the years they'd played together previously. By the time they were on to their last song, it was almost as if they'd never quit.

They ended on a crescendo of sound: Dex playing sixteenths, Suzi's trumpet sustaining a high note, Javier noodling extemporaneously on the keys, Arvind going to town on the drums while Kandace mixed it all with loops and distortion into something approaching magic. When Javier nodded for the final note, Dex felt a flush of joy flow throughout his body. The audience, which he'd left on for both sound and vision, broke into applause which crashed over him like a wave. There really was nothing quite like playing live, even if it was technically a simulation.

He and the rest of the band shared a drink at the bar after, laughing and deconstructing their performance. A few audience members stopped by to chat and a couple of additional rounds were somehow acquired. After nearly an hour, though, the crowd thinned out and Dex saw a table full of familiar faces.

"You were great, honey," Annabelle said, standing to give him a kiss.

"Just like old times." Dex turned at the sound of a familiar voice to see the avatar of his old friend and musical partner, Maks. "I'm a little jealous, over here." He grinned and gave Dex a hug.

"Nothing stopping you," Dex said. "There's always room for more tunes."

Maks nodded and lifted his glass in a toast.

"Good to see you playing again, Dex."

"Thanks, Captain." Zahara Zhang had been a regular at Chemical Celeste's gigs in the past, so Dex wasn't terribly surprised to see her.

"That was nowhere near as painful as I'd feared it might be."

"René?" Biagini had always avoided Dex's gigs before, whether in the physical world or the virtual. It was, as he'd explained before, not his scene, but Dex guessed his friend realized how much this night meant to him.

"You are a man of many talents." René's eerily generic avatar smiled and Dex tried but failed to see in it an echo of his friend. The voice was right, though, and the warmth in it was as genuine as anything. "It makes me wish to speculate on what other skills you are keeping under wraps."

"Wouldn't you like to know," Annabelle said, looping her arm through Dex's. Captain Zhang pretended to not have heard the exchange, but everyone else laughed.

"Oh, it's been a long time," Dex said, sighing.

"Too long," Maks said and waved over a bot waiter for another round of drinks.

MOST BARS AND PUBLIC spaces in M City never closed — between global timezones and twenty-four hour shiftwork, it's always beer o'clock for someone — but the crowd at the Sidetrack had thinned out considerably. Maks had begged off, after extracting a promise from Dex to do a better job of keeping in touch. René had another engagement lined up and made his excuses, leaving Annabelle, Dex and Captain Zhang on their own. They stayed at the bar, but switched to a private encrypted voice channel. It probably wasn't necessary but it was habit by now.

Dex gave Zhang a brief rundown on the conversation he'd had with Kora at the warehouse. "I've reexamined the history of your inherited disk block," he said, "and while I have no way to prove that it went down like this, I'm reasonably convinced that Irina Nightingale probably spent a few years very carefully acquiring a bunch of disk blocks from Oyuba. From what I can tell, it was all done on the up and up, but resulted in her personally controlling a small firm's worth of rez space."

"That's some impressive skimming work," Zhang said.

"Is it really skimming if you actually pay for it?" Annabelle asked.

Zhang shrugged. "I guess not, but I'm assuming that we're talking about cents on the euro here, right? I mean, what would be the point if you're paying market rate?"

"None," Dex said, "but the impression I get from my source is that this is typical. You know what they say, only suckers pay retail."

Annabelle made a face. "Yeah, 'suckers' — which is pretty much everyone who doesn't have some kind of inside connection."

"Maybe that's part of what Nightingale was trying to do," Zhang said, "open up those inside connections. "

"I guess you could say that's what we're all trying to do," Dex said. "The system is rigged, designed to benefit the people and companies that already have power, influence and money. It's a feed-forward system. The poor stay poor and the rich get rich. It's no secret; everybody knows that's the way it is — the problem is that so many people have bought into the lie that if they play the game and follow the rules, they might get to be the one in a million who makes the jump."

"Looks like Nightingale did," Zhang said.

"Maybe," Dex said. "Who knows how she started out, though. She had to have been somewhat higher on the pecking order to do what she did."

"And at least she decided in the end to change the rules," Annabelle said. "Like we all did in here, when we took the power away from the companies who were trying to control M City. They thought they could take their pay to play model and bring it online, where we'd always been able to freely share information. Did they really think that people wouldn't fight back?"

"I guess they figured that we'd all be used to it by now," Zhang said.

"Like we are out there," Dex said. The three of them sat in silence for a moment, lost in their individual thoughts.

"It's not going to be as easy to get people to fight in the physical world as it was in here," Annabelle said. "So many of us gave up on that space a long time ago. That's why we fought back in here — this was our place. Somewhere you could be the person who wasn't allowed to exist out there. Even a person who would never disobey an order or even push back against their boss would be willing to fight for that. But out there..." She got a faraway look in her eyes. "To so many people, out there is a lost cause. It's a necessary evil — the job, the food, the body."

Zhang nodded. "It's hard to fight for something you don't feel belongs to you."

"Well, then, maybe that's the key," Dex said. "To try and get people to remember that it all belongs to them. The virtual and the physical, both."

"That's going to be tough," Annabelle said. "People are afraid out there. Afraid of losing a job and with it access to everything they need to survive. Afraid of being harassed or worse if they are on the street or working on their own. You can believe in the need for change with every cycle of your system but if it comes between living your beliefs and keeping a job you need — most people will opt for the status quo every time."

"That's the problem," Zhang said. "The people are afraid, but that's not how it should be. The firms, their shareholders, they don't really have the power. Sure, they can make or break an individual employee, but without all those employees, all those consumers, they don't have anything. Without us, they have no market."

"We have the power, but we only have it together." Dex wasn't sure if this thought made him feel hopeful or despondent. "How can we possibly get people to stop being afraid?"

"That's been the question for all of human history, hasn't it?" Zhang said. "It's how every conqueror has triumphed, how every dictator keeps their throne."

"I guess all we can do is show that there's another way," Dex said. "To walk unafraid, to work for a fairer system even when it's inconvenient. To try and be who we really are both in this world of light and out there in the sun."

They clicked their glasses in a toast, a sense of purpose settling over the conversation. Dex knew his little speech sounded good, might even win over one or two people, but he also knew that it was so much easier to say than it was to do. To just stop being afraid — if it were only that simple, they'd all have done it long ago.

Because they were all afraid. Himself, Annabelle, even Captain Zhang. They all just pressed that feeling down, or pushed through it, to do what they had to in spite of it.

Maybe that was the real secret.

Being afraid, but acting anyway.

Acknowledgments

Thanks to Eileen Gunnell Lee for the excellent comments on an early draft of this book.

I also owe the people from my various online writing homes a great debt for everything. Special thanks go to my patrons on Patreon, who literally made this book a reality.

And always, thanks to Steven, who makes everything a reality.

ABOUT THE AUTHOR

Darusha writes science fiction and speculative poetry as M. Darusha Wehm and mainstream poetry and fiction as Darusha Wehm. Science fiction books include: *Beautiful Red*, *Children of Arkadia* and the Andersson Dexter cyberpunk detective series. Mainstream books include the Devi Jones' Locker Young Adult series and *The Home for Wayward Parrots* (forthcoming from NeWest Press).

Darusha's short fiction and poetry have appeared in many venues, including *Arsenika*, *Nature*, *Escape Pod*, and several anthologies.

Darusha is originally from Canada but currently lives in Wellington, New Zealand after spending the past several years sailing the Pacific.

For more information, visit http://darusha.ca.